Tenement Press 4, MMXXII
ISBN 978-1-8380200-6-4

CW01432018

MUEUM
SJ Fowler

A showcase, ransacked with horrid delight: Fowler's *MUEUM* presents the placid, lurid violences of surveillance and exhibition with startling and brutal stylishness. A seething triumph.
    —Eley Williams

Down in the mire of London's grimpen, above the drained marshlands and drift of the fatbergs, exist the cultural centres that shine like jewels in the mudcake of the greatest city on earth: London's museums. Their great domes are craniums through which pass the crazy, unbidden thoughts of a culture always moving closer to madness.

    With the apocalyptic vision of Ballard and the acerbic attitude of Céline, *MUEUM* scatters human detritus over the shiny Perspex of our most dearly loved vitrines. Rimbaud's visits to the British Museum reading room come to mind: scratching himself down for lice as he flicked through the latest encyclopaedias. And Bataille, assembling curios so strange the Surrealists wouldn't touch them wearing gloves.

    MUEUM is a novel of watchers and the watched, a testament to the fact that people are always more interesting—and far stranger—than things. And nothing is stranger than people's obsession with touching objects from the questionable past.

    Prepare to travel the world, from Rome to Japan, with a travelling troupe of unforgettable characters who walk the world each day but never leave a building. SJ Fowler's *MUEUM* is an essential artefact for our troubled times, proving that travel of the mind is always more powerful than the real thing.
    —Chris McCabe

SJ Fowler is arguably the most influential, tirelessly generative and expansively generous English artist working in experimental literature today. No other contemporary writer is as comprehensively, and ambitiously, engaged with Europe's histories of the avant-garde in addition to such vital participation in its present. Whether in poetry, essays, fiction, painting, scrawling, sculpting, film, performance, theatre, sound, or in happenings without definition, his art draws its volatile experience of language into the mobile and embodied possibility of language as experience. Emerging in feral exploration between the poetry of Tom Raworth and the prose of László Krasznahorkai, this is a shape-shifting and omnivorous body of writing; uncompromisingly alive in the playful, violent, oblique and confrontational.
    —David Spittle

A book as powerful, monumental and strange as Alasdair Gray's *Lanark* in miniature.
    —Joanna Walsh

MUEUM

And yet this drowning in space was accompanied by an extra-ordinary rise of the concrete, we were in the cosmos, but as though we were in something terrifyingly definite, determined in every detail.
    —Witold Gombrowicz

You can get a sudden attack of nausea by staying too long in an art gallery as well. It must be some kind of illness—museumitis—unknown to medical science. Or could it be the air of death surrounding all things man-made, whether beautiful or ugly?
    —Gustav Heyrink

I

Between 6am and 8am surges pour onto the city, killing everyone still there and smashing remaining buildings. Things collapse for the last time and darkness spreads across the province.

The cloud reaches its peak and unleashes a crushing density of bones, expelled from its back end. This causes the widespread collapse of certain buildings. It affects the future; birth rates and so forth; and triggers the deadly surge to begin again. The fog emits noxious gas and unearthly noises and there are violent tremors. Some people escape into a river. Back into the city, the sounds of scribbled signatures is heard everywhere.

Ash and pumice rains down and by the late afternoon, the city is smothered. People are trapped by blocked doors or by ceilings and roofs collapsing under the weight. This is where we arrive, later on, when we're squared up, immaculate. We pass through the plaster walls easily.

After more small explosions the main surge is kaput. Yet a small mushroom cloud of superheated metal blows southwards killing everyone who had fled to the river and plunging everything into even darker darkness. Some sort of delayed reaction. A plant, or foundry, going up. No one knows. The metal had formed natural bunkers in the earth and we were able to move on upon them, leaving our amputees and assorted wounded to clean up after us, often nested in a divot.

It was not the darkness of a cloudy night or a night where there is no moon. But darkness as if the light has gone out in a room that is locked and sealed. A deep ocean darkness, above water. You could see all around you on that horrible land the shrieks of people, the wailing of infants, and the shouting of men. Who died first? Who last? Who was left to care? It was a time of petty revenge, and relative discretion. The dead were the heroes of their own stories, legends of their own bathtubs. The living were unexpected.

As the rebuilding began, all scores settled, so it's said that our cutting off of taste has some part in what is lost, but that this is necessary. For the manifestations of human intellectual achievement regarded collectively were not there to hold onto when things took place.

Acknowledged by all who live is that there is a plan to this, in earth's experience, but that we are quite mere in it. The best we can do is do our best to put objects in houses. Then look at them. Then remember. Then see ourselves in it all.

Culture begins in the history we rebuild.

History begins in the Museum rebuilt.

II

Fruitless orchard lines the graceless square barricade of the blockade. It stops the crowd amassing and overwhelming the gate. Planted from memory, from some gardeners' notes, a re-collection of blueprints, is the line of tall, absolutely un-tropical, trees. They are oddly tall, like certain people, swaying above even the spiked tip of the obstruction doors. They have foliage only upon their upper reaches, where it's too high for men to climb. In that regard there has been fidelity to how it used to be. Outside the first Museum. Old we might say, rather than first. Who can say what Museum was first? That is for a Museum of Museums. Something likely to be on its way.

The trees slough their dander down upon the queues, and into the courtyard, onto the staff and public alike. Though they aren't alike, in countenance or conduct. In tiny insectoid woollen stars the spores of these trees come down and cling to rough cloth. They also find their way, in miniscule shards, like hairs on a fish, onto the fingers, skin and eyes of the lucky. For many, in doing so, they cause red eye, hacking coughs and irresistible itching. The trees have been implanted in memory of the trees. Practicalities be damned. It has been mooted that were they once replaced with plastic replicas, that their rain had irritated the wrong curator. Plastic trees would still harbour the past. I can see the argument. Some say sacrilege, and controversy. But there would then be no consequence for human health. So, what would be the point? To just be observed, to be looked at? For the public to say, this is what they looked like? Rather than, this is what they are?

It occurs to me they are plastic, and there is a machine, or machines inside, which produce the fluff. The idea makes me satisfied, because what a creative thought that is. And what kind of toxicity that would produce—using that word properly. But one step at a time, we're not at the *'what's worst for human health above all other factors'* stage quite yet. We're getting there. The fact is, do we know why the original Museum would've have planted such painful, ugly trees?

Particulars are not the worry.

In the forecourt, before the gate, flanked by our barracks, and leading to the main entrance, clumps of inane-in-appearance bushes line the curves of gardens and circle the iced surfaces of the mostly hidden ponds. No fences surround them. We get a few pleasant splashes per day. The bushes are there to listen. See what the chatter is on the way in. I am young, but old enough to know when they were inert. The microphones are not well disguised, and that is the point. If you see them, then you are seen looking.

We go out into the courtyard for our breakfast every day, in a very strict routine. It's every day we do that. Ideal, to eat early. We wait until the trees have ceased their shedding. There is a small guard shed to shelter, if it is brutally cold, as it often is, during a season or two. Our house, as it's known, the barracks, is white, with two floors and a mansard roof. It is surrounded by firs and thuyas, flowerbeds and paths, which are plastic, and once dumbfounded us all, individually, like a historical vision. We were used to nothing, when each of us got our jobs here, as guards.

When we first laid eyes upon these places and plants, some thought them a mirage, those that had been on the teams. But, as I've always said, hallucinations tend to fade. It's not like things are bad enough for them to be necessary. As they were when we were doing that work, cleaning things up, getting our hands grubby. Before the antagonisms this would have been nothing. But over time their permanence makes them seem more real than they are. The feeling that they are not true, that they are at odds, is afforded only to the nostalgic. Those who cling to a notion of the organic and artificial. Which seems, to me, spoiled. I suppose this is the point of plastic flowers.

We guards are sat around small circular tables, eating. Here comes a visitor host, in a green jacket. At first, they are waving to us, in the distance, so they don't cause alarm. You never can tell. There is a friendly repartee between the guards and the hosts. Green jackets and orange jackets. There is some gentle mockery, some industrial enmity. But not a real rivalry, really. Guards are guards, mostly ex-service, with some civilians recently, as we die out, and visitor hosts are what they are without a specific and notable previous career. They are chosen because of their willingness to be pliable in the face of cataclysmic human rudeness.

This host is careful. She asks if we slept well? We are all with pink eyes from lack and the older guards murmur as they young smile. The dead of night last night crosses my mind, but no one, including me, wants to hear about my dreams. Some people don't even have them or say they don't remember them. The visitor host continues to chat idly, about the gateway, and the fields and the sweep of country, as she calls it, gesturing be-hind her, to nothing in particular. A little wind kicks up with her, she Is talking about production, how many visitors they expect today. She glosses over. In her hand is a little, hardened clump of mud. It looks like it has passed through a worm. She works it finely between her fingers, never breaking it from a bubble. I am repelled, as is intended, by her growing enthusiasm. I won-der where she found that clod? She is a program worker, an early riser, she has probably been up and about for hours already. Not ingenious enough to be a curator. In her defense, she looks as though she has recovered from a dire illness. She flaunts her jacket and swipes her thin hands around us all as she talks over the older guards. How familiar she seems, between plastic flow-ers, to loom above us. Her eyes peep out like lumps on a bent plate, all milky, the same soft colour as those horrid dreams we don't have. She casts a brief glance over me, and smiles, nodding to approve of my shape. She has fake rabbit skins on her belt, hanging from ear to tail, ready to be bunched by the lengthy ears in her outstretched grip for a tour or live display. She will likely play a Neolithic hunter today, or maybe a Roman. The plastic rabbits are bound up with a red bow. Weird she looks at me so intently, I feel miffed for a moment. I won't show it, just in case the others think it means more than it might. So much gossip. Nothing to it, I would never even prolong a conversation with a host. Soon she obviously begins to consider her gestures point-less and withdraws her hand. Then she is gone, I lose track of how because Greg is sat next to me, moving a bit.

What's her name again? Someone asks.

We amble through another morning. It strikes me that everything, although it remains the same, is not. Not a novel idea. One that's regular, when I think of myself thinking. I have the urge to write it down. Today is different. To write down: today is unusual. That would be odd too, to write as though my particular feeling might be worth recording and not to then write, today is different because I am writing down today is different. As though menial work—endless, taskless, almost pointless labour might be the subject, for noticing change. Not in this world or any before it, where people are employed to displace space and suffer the depredations of indirect danger.

Beside me sits Greg, his long aimless face caught by the illumination of the massive courtyard lamps that are being craned into place by engineers, readying for the opening. It lights him in such a way that I can perceive the fine details of his face, and that's not good, as anyone who has had to have sex from the front will attest. He looks like a nice crocodile. The hairs growing from within his noise, curling their way out of his nostrils, the splayed pores of his cheeks, the wet edges of his lips, the shell in his eyes. Greg is bent, dripping into his food bowl, round shouldered, in his blue collared shirt, his clipped tie and his black hewn trousers, Museum logo stamped upon the arse cheek. His mouth trembles with each mouthful. A typical demoted intellectual, a less typical survivor, the opposite of that visitor host. Just grateful for food and lodgings and things to see. What he must have seen, people's spread, the slow destruction of skeletons. Worse than me really. It's certainly easier to be watched than watch. You can control the tempo etcetera. I don't know. Something has affected him. It's hard to escape seeing him all limp. He means well.

From Greg to the gates, all seems indebted to an awkward rampancy, an innocent success. Maybe it's a weekend. We can see the public, like a raring set of harmless dogs. The queue is bunching here and there, through the railings. Once we were outside too. The materials seemed continual then, as though the Museum was fashioned as one piece and had always been so. That is the point. Just as Greg, and many of my other colleagues, seemed timeless when I first met them. A fatiguing thought, that these bags of jaws were once unknown to me.

Greg behaved so well. I nudged him right off, intending to express to him what had happened to me in solidarity with his distant stare, but he placed his finger to his lips. What a relief. That's the last impressive thing he has done. I suggest to him he give his face another wash before our shift begins.

That would be no use today, he murmurs, and I think this a weird thing to mutter.

He vanishes into the guard's house like it were a cave.

You should wash again, I repeat, after him, trying to calm him down a bit.

Greg is not popular. They others, they neglect him.

He's too clever for his own good, they say. Perhaps what I have perceived in him is that our paths are inverse. That he begins, his life and each day, with a loud channel he must quiet. We normally sit in silence upon a bench dedicated to a dead guard. Usually, he is absorbed entirely in himself and for just for a moment, before we have to stand and go inside, his face clears up. Greg comes back and smiles. Breakfast is coming to an end. He won't sit again; it hurts his legs to squat. He says something plainly intended to make his presence bearable, less oppressive. I realise how precarious it is to be sitting with him like this, where his awkward and accidental insistence on eccentricity can be noticed, surrounded by the other guards, who reflect their work so physically it is seeping into their cells like leprosy. Men whose joints creak and whose jagged faces remain impassive amidst the dreadful and indulgent behaviour of the public, and amongst whom Greg is a whimpering, sensitive apparition. At some point the stone engulfs all the physical material in a guard, at some cumulative moment, the endless hours guarding peak and the body loses its substantive fleshiness. Quite the opposite of being what I was before. The workless work will render the body nearly invisible, veiled, remaining behind a caul. With all the menace of a thin cap of skin over a human face too, it leaves the guards perhaps better suited to their work. Greg must have realised this as he almost shoos me away from him, like I was a big pigeon, because he's increasingly animated today, in the details. There's something going on. I never saw him so significant.

The floodlights brighten. We all stand up. I see the immobility come over them. I look down the line. Time has come. The sound of shoes.

Off to work, Greg murmurs.

What d'you mean? I reply, speaking to his back.

III

The morning courtyard is full of hosts and guards, builders
and gritters, accidentally, criss-crossing, muttering under their
breaths, ignoring it in each other, preserving it in themselves,
buttoning their coats and checking their devices as they go. Dust
is up out of the building itself, settling in after door-opening.
It mixes with the slough. I'm itching at my legs and the floor is
slippery. A man behind me seems to skid and just about right
himself. I feel a hard budge as he turns, trying to overcompen-
sate. He touches my shoulder and I spin, falling and getting up.
No one can stop to help me. I examine my uniform, partially
stained with grit, below my elbow and below my knee. I slap at
the marks.

Keep your balance. A woman's voice. It is not the man who
felled me. I see him leave. The woman is artificially lowering her
tone. It is not at all amusing. Shut your face. I retort, not initially
recognising the voice of Rebecca.

Keep up, she insists.

For a moment Rebecca hovers before me, even though I
have stood upright. As if she could catch me and hold my weight,
as though I was about to fall again. She then ignores me. As
is normal.

Have you got your posts? I ask, to keep her near.

She brushes herself to imitate me, or to mock me. In a
blunt, leaden way, as with so many of my colleagues. But then,
her and I have been close, so this may have more substance.

Of course. I'm on my way in, she says, pointing to the
building. I feel jealous.

I don't have mine, I say.

I snap for want of saying something else, gesturing to
no one in particular within the moving mass. Ideally, I'd enjoy
her staying still, so I can admit to a recent, illogical jealousy.
We have not been assigned adjacent galleries for quite some
time. Nothing unusual in that being unusually. It's quite possibly accidental, and not her, or someone else, calling in a favour.
You wonder what you have done. You check yourself for odours.
Our once regular meetings in The Enlightenment Gallery were
noteworthy. We were temporarily close up. Biting the inside
of my lip, she once caught my gum with her tooth, because we
couldn't see, inside a cupboard, and it makes a truthful impression that this feeling of intimacy doesn't linger when
the original experience of that affection felt transient. If not
a transition, then a regretful episode. It just wasn't there,

as I've heard other people say. But if it is not actually there, well I could do with a person to look at, to look through, to look with. Her face is salting up just encountering me. One wonders what we have done to offend people. But my wonder doesn't stretch too far. I am a horrible plank, so awful it is every time I act. It plagues the mind, how I appear to others, like a missing tooth. Just to keep safe, when we have met since we stopped meeting, I barely speak a word.

What? she says, mimicking me, before answering my question.

It is eight-forty-five. So?

How many in the Museum present to others their symptoms as a kind of familial love. I could be her brother; such is her lack of control. Incest in The Enlightenment Gallery. One of the many unspoken and regular occurrences of every history, no matter how many times its looped round. Two people, stuck in a box, are they really going to think of the genes?

Rebecca would say she was out in the field before all this, not with me, but with another team. And because she had no choice, not because she wanted to be clearing houses. As though we aren't all always teaching ourselves to enjoy it, and making the best of it, and remembering it better than it was. She's too good for that. She actually regrets it. As though we had a choice. How convenient is choice in the mind... Back to incest. Had she ended up on one side or another by accident, I might've been the one to ensure she wasn't here now. I've seen Rebecca slap a child full in the face, getting some ear with the cheek. I've seen her peel fingers from statues and give them a sordid tug. I've seen her prep herself to have hollow eye sockets, with some sort of make-up caving around the eyeballs. I've seen her bark orders, and clear galleries like an unrepentant murderer. I have seen her eat without chewing, rushing back to post, and push weaker people, men and women, aside, before they were removed. She is a very loud quiet colleague. In the cupboard, once, or even twice, she would have miniaturised breakdowns, afterward, and pull tufts of my pubic hair out, unexpectedly, or even attempt to grab and squeeze my testicles. I barely remember. She is in the Museum not because she had no choice but precisely the opposite. And not just in the Museum, in the Blue Team. She, like Greg, is curious because almost no one else needs to be. She's tall like Greg too.

They must get a lot of stares from the visitors.

In boasting that I have not got my posts; I realise I haven't. This is the first time I am without them, and this makes me anxious. I appreciate that this is why I have been apprehensive. My thoughts are chaining away today. We normally, as in every day ever, go and fetch our posts before we eat breakfast. We wake, wash, dress, raise our places and then return to eat. I have never broken this routine. How has it been possible to forget? I knuckle my own head to rake the brain inside. How is it I found myself eating breakfast without knowing where I will work today? The time is alarming. I couldn't have been late getting up, I had sat with Greg and the guards. I have made a mess of the order. I had sat there, fresh from shower. Something has become. I really don't wish to claim it's internal. I am not suffering the signs of traumatic disorder. Any longer. Any more than anyone else. Any more than usual. *Calm*. I repeat myself. It crosses my lips amiably. I am calm. Yes, that's right. I must get my posts.

Action over inaction.

Through the crowd I pass and push. The Post Office better still be functioning as it is officially supposed to, until nine. Or I'm going to have to tell someone. But who would I tell? We supervise ourselves, apart from the curators. I can't tell a curator something so trivial and stupid. Nine is the time we have to be on our posts. Ten to nine is when the curator, whichever one is the one today, addresses us. I have, at best, four minutes to make it through the Post Office, fetch my note and return to The Great Hall. This all seems unlikely. My knees and elbows ache from falling.

Out of the crowd, toward the building. I feel for my pass. It is not round my neck. Where is my lanyard? Finding it in my pocket I examine the picture. It seems reasonable to check it is my face beneath the laminate. I'm convinced. An old picture, the first day at the Museum, seven years ago. Every year they update the pass, on the same date, our Museum birthday, but not the picture. To remind us? That we were once desperate for this work. We were thinner. Ironically, though I was near mal-nourishment, my face is fatter in the photo, with heavier cheeks and a thicker neck. My hair oiled back, so it wouldn't get in my eyes when I was doing what I was doing. I look older than I am now. I look ready-to-work, rather than worked. I don't look calm. Yet I remember I could've gone on forever like that. I don't remember feeling hopeless. I wasn't wounded anywhere. Or was this a dream from last night? This brings comfort, that

I am now none the less lean, fitter, more youthful. I look at the tiny face before me. A future is in my humourlessness and compliance. If one believes in a cyclical hypothesis of history. Seems as convincing as anything else. I think that was an early trial name for the Museum. The Museum of History. Or was it the Museum of Futures? The Museum of Debt. I don't know, I saw it written in one of the basement galleries once, I think. Putting my cord around my neck, I check my pockets for anything else I might've left behind.

Breaking the crowd is inevitably conspicuous, but it doesn't seem I've been seen. The guards are going or have gone into The Great Hall, as are the others to their posts or cubes or fixes. I approach the Post Office, on the far side of the courtyard, opposite the Barracks. Two long hangars brace the courtyard, which leads to the Main Building and The Great Hall and the Galleries of the Museum. The courtyard draws the public into the slender front tip of the Museum, as it also hides these wings that stand stout like sentinels. I know nothing of this wing but the PO, and the staff garden that almost no one ever uses, because of its distance from the galleries. Apart from that, I know nothing. There must be a hundred rooms in this building. Storage. A place for the objects that didn't quite fit this Museum. They say, the Post Office has been placed as far away from the Barracks as possible so we have to walk in front of the main entrance of the Museum every morning. To make us exercise, or so they can see us as we cross. There's plenty of places in the entrance where one could spy, with its arches and massive stone carving of an unidentified human, sporting a headdress, half sunk, half jutting from the pinnacle of the portico, is all in soapy green stone. The statue, famously, is cut to the waist, shirtless, indistinct features chiselled, uneroded, but still somehow muted. The blade of a weapon is in his ribs with hands around its hilt but no body behind the hands. They used to kill them like that. Something I did see. This big anonymous blundering person represents them knowing what people like to see. He is like the second child, a fall back, coming to be a statue. Its eyes are without pupils, no little awkward pearls in the stone. It is looking ahead of itself, or looking nowhere, about to be slashed in half. Perhaps it was blind, or its expression is masking a rare illness. It looks like the statue is clutching a small knife with a gold

's a small snake. Little use such a weapon would do you.

ee as you get close. Greg says it wasn't a person, that

the statue is a symbol. But I think he's being a bit literal and don't mind saying so. Smartarses don't always go far.

At the PO there is no obvious door if you don't know where to look. It stops the public coming in. In the unlikely event they have wandered from the queue running gate to door and not been immediately bashed in the head by someone like me. They are happy to be roped back as they are heading into the Galleries. The Museum contains many doors to be discovered closed but outer doors simply require inside knowledge, and it's just their handles that are hidden. I touch the wall to find the crease. I pass the walking tunnel that I believe leads to the staff garden. Suddenly a man emerges. He nearly bumps into me.

Where are you going? He says.

Who are you? I reply, as abrupt as his appearance.

Sorry, he says. You couldn't be seen there.

Are you ill? I ask, for the garden is often where the sick go and a point must always be made.

I am, he says, and pulling back from me, I can see he is.

Off to bed then, I say, just to get him off me.

That is where I am going, he replies.

I let him go. In trying to remember his face I realise I have never seen it before. His jumper is laughably large, many sizes too big for him. His hands are inside the sleeves, shrunk in the folds of cloth. I turn back and touch the wall past the bins and refuse bay and the incinerator, which creates a stench, and plays no small part in waking us up every morning. It has the authority of an earth smell, though it is just burnt wood and rust, and plastic. I discover the word STAFF etched into the brick, almost hidden for the shallowness of the carving and the colour of the stone.

I hesitate on an impulse to turn back. Being without my posts may be the lesser of evils. The doors are heavy, I push them open and am in the cold corridor with a ceiling so squat a very tall man would have to duck. Crouching I become aware it is not as low as I had expected. I stand again and peer down the hall. I had not remembered its awkward dimensions, never having been in the space isolated. The ninth door. I count, feeling a foot of space above my head. The eight other doors have only keyholes. At the ninth I give out a middle knuckle for a gentle rap. No noise from within, nor an echo. I doubt I have made a sound and knock again, impatiently. I look to my right and left. The corridor stretches elsewhere. A retreat to the

courtyard soon, preparing excuses, which will be a reprieve
from this waiting. One more knock, and again nothing. I lean
forward and the door just opens, cushioning my weight. An
empty room with blue plastic waiting benches and a counter.
Lights illuminate, automatically. From the counter, a grunt.

May I come in? I ask. Don't mind me, I say.

The proper protocol for approaching the clerk when on
time is difficult enough. I hold my pass in my pocket. I step
towards, rude, like a visitor, like something being deliberately
dropped.

You are lucky I am here, says the man.

He is alert, furrowed, staring right into me, as though
he had been waiting, as though I had broken his line of sight.
He sits up on a stool, back perfectly straight, legs before him,
feet resting on a brace, hands on knees. I recognise him,
but I think not from the Post Office.

Were you just outside? I ask.

Mate, he says.

Don't you normally work here?

You are lucky, he says again, I'm gone by now.

He seems to incline his head, but not because of what I
feel is an ongoing and gradually comforting conversation. I have
the sense he knows I am fortunate to be getting posts given
what I've done and I feel he is about to remind me of what kind
of person he thinks I am. Everything in the past was filmed of
course. It's just no one knows how to watch the footage anymore.
Or so we think.

You're here for your posts.

It is not a question.

I think of words like 'colleague,' 'comrade,' 'friend.'

My name is...

Yes yes. I see you every bastard day mate.

He flips open a ledger that has sat on the desk between us
and that I hadn't noticed. His rapidity of movement, and his
sheer and continued neutrality is becoming of his position and
his grumpy punishment is losing its effect through familiarity.

You're not down to work, he says.

I feel nauseous. Am I seeing a smile on him?

You're not down to work today. Your name is not on
the brief.

I have worked, and been upon that brief, for 2559 days,
I insist.

I've no recollection of that indicating what is to happen after it, he says.

That is definitely a nod. Not a smile. A tilt. He moves away as though to consult some record, off to his left, my eyes watering, unable to focus on the speed of his fingers. He seems to find something.

You're okay mate, he says, without weight or deference.

What?

You're alright. Go on.

Go on where? I've got like two minutes...

I know, I know. Go on, they'll have something for you to do.

Back to the...

Back to work.

He shuts his ledge and I turn and flee the way I have come, like a proper coward.

IV

Nobody speaks at muster. The Great Hall ceiling is glass, and today, muggy and obscured. We must assume this is the weather above. That's enough to look at. But no one looks up as they enter and join their teams, and muster. To keep employees quiet as they move there are electric lights too, for no other reason I can discern. Today, as with every day, the two giant staircases of The Great Hall are littered with the dull green ground of workers descending to their stations. Guards are spreading to their rooms. Greeters are prepping their bodies, straightening their collars, straightening their faces, and the visitor hosts, overseen by the curator, are scampering, to begin their fabrications. I know what they do down there. Before I became a guard I knew. I impressed upon them I was too large and impatient for the work. I sabotaged myself. It would hurt my feelings to see the things being made. From pictures in books. From imaginations. Being visionary is no good for me. Too much mud in the water. When I get my hands on ideas, I am less steady. And I couldn't be a host, those at the other end. The ones who speak to the public. I'd harm them. In unacceptable volumes. That's why I became a Guard of the Galleries, though I shouldn't pretend I chose. A guard. With less requirements.

I slip by myself to join my team. I have not been spotted nor have I been aware of evasion. I am now standing with Team Blue. There are catering staff still crossing the hall too, so I'm not that late. They are the only ones I see can see me. They are the most anonymous. Working in the cafes and restaurants too numerous to count, being perceptive. They are not even polite. Something else. And nobody cares what they see, so I'm fine. They are like the cleaners. Where they come from, I don't know, but half of them have missing parts. Survivors, that's for sure. Many have been here longer than me, living off some obscure charity. Or so it would appear.

Blue Team seems to have not noticed my absence, nor now my presence. For seven years I've mustered. Before being sent to guard things in rooms. Muster, and then I stand still, in rooms called galleries. That is the work. To displace volume with my body and not sleep. I have done little but be in this time. It has been steady. And in that a kind of *no*. A kindness too. I have felt, but not seen, the world settle in. My rooms have become placid. I have written hundreds of short letters about this. Foot notes. At first destroying them, then folding them, and now, as things have relaxed, stacking them in a corner, beneath my bed. They do not form an account. And everyone knows. They know I might've written one, a record. But they'd just put that on display. Nameless of course. A biography or something. But I do not mention the past. And what could I say of the future? And the present cumulates into featurelessness. There is no account. Which pleases them. It's not worth their trusting a sought-after spot to someone accounting when they should be just standing. They let me scribble. They think it offsets my other predilections. Not only harmless but useful. That's a theory they manage by. Allow a little to save a lot. As long as the writing isn't complete. Inconclusive, not consistent. Not all sense. They have a little black heart to let me compose. Mostly it isn't words. It's like words. I'm literate. It's my handwriting. They probably think I'm trying to write a new language for them. To pretend it's from the past. And they know it is seven hard years of serving at the feet of an unpredictable brutishness. One that cannot be pre- dicted, and avoided, and now, cannot be lost. That is the dread crowd. The dead hands. The visitors. The public. I have come to know the Museum as one enormous case against people col- lecting in groups. And that is why I scribble my notes. For that is the record of the crowd. And it is all even worse if they gather to just look. At things.

The morning address must have happened. I must've missed it. The team begins the walk to their posts just as I take up the back end. The problem remains, I have no place to go. The ebb of Greg, Rebecca, Kevin, Terry, also Thomas, Andy, Andrew, Onion, Linn, Pat, James, it gives me something to do. I follow. Something I'm used to. My team is a loose gang. Experts at actively milling. Professional draggers of the feet. But not to be underestimated. They are now going in and on as slowly as possible and I fall by without drawing attention to my speed. I observe them more keenly today, still disturbed they might

know something that I do not know, about myself. I realise
I am something like proud to be with them. Pleased. Pleased
to be team blue. We were long ago assigned teams with colour
codes. We had no say in it. But once you are with your team, you
are with them, or you are leaving the Museum. We meet other
teams, we are allowed to meet them, when it is informally done,
at break and lunch. But this all has the appearance of being very
informal. There are no strictures on being compatriots with
our colleagues in team Silver say, or the Red team. Quite a few
ex-service on Blue. Though we are not officially allowed to talk
on the Galleries, especially about the old days, we do. I know
them as well as they can be known.

     We are each assigned our own gallery. Four per day. Or
a space within a larger room. We are supposed to exchange only
official information, or warnings. We control the shape of our
mouths as we speak. We speak for great lengths in the gallery
canteen. The older guards tell me this was made up by the first
guards of the new Museum, who based it, so they say, on the
vernacular of the old Museum. Seems unlikely. They tell me this
with their hands covering their lips. The first guards of the new
Museum were martial, like me, but older. They were lifers being
retired, military as a vocation, not conscripts or opportunists.
We were probably doing the same things, but I was younger
doing it. And it took me a few years longer to come in. Or so
they say. The visitors then were probably quite different. Quite
polite possibly, or so it seems from the pictures. It was different
on the outside then, I'd bet. Not all the younger staff learn the
talk, but I have. I can rattle on for hours without detection.
Not all see the need.

We are walking to the south-east corner of the Hall. A few short today, when I scan heads. The Great Hall has few objects, but we are mulling past the statue of Elagabalus. The dull Roman corner. His parts are missing. One of the new, temporary workers has been let go and they are talking about him. I would've been the news, otherwise. I read their lips; it is Mark. Mark is gone. Ironic they are talking of him in code, the older ones, who never really spoke to him anyway. Nor I really. We could all see he wouldn't last long. Mark was deluding himself. I knew he didn't know what he needed to know, to be squared away. You need to play the long game. I'm just beginning, seven years in, for example, so they tell me. Mark had it just built, the Museum, standing tall, in his mind, from the first day. It's true he looked old, but he wasn't. He was born after the revision, whatever you want to call it, our cycle beginning. Or he was a child during. Whatever the case, Guarding was a chance for him to have some thinking time he said, and at that, a gentle wave from me as I walked off. Poor lad. The exact opposite is the case, he had no time to think, because time isn't filled with thought. Not automatically. I know more than most, you need something before the time to let the *it* happen. A scribble or so. Otherwise, it isn't thinking the time. It's a lot worse.

It occurs to me, maybe my post is what his post was to be? But this isn't the system, so it'd be the first time such a weird swap had happened. Usually, the procedure is simple. There are eleven teams and the Museum is divided into eleven sections. Each section is not necessarily formed into a section because of its content, that is its objects and the civilisations these objects represent, both real and new. Fire safety is the reason for the system, they say, which is important, to me at least, given the obvious risk of things burning. When the fire shutters fall, then it's important to know why they have eleven teams in eleven sections. Within each section there is thirty-three posts. That means there is near enough thirty-three galleries, but some galleries are so large as to contain multiple posts. The eleven sections sit on seven levels. Naturally there are three above the Great Hall and three below. Yet there are more, below, more levels, but they do not contain currently accessible galleries. There have been claims, for as long as I have worked in the Museum, that the minus four level galleries will be one day opened. This seems unlikely. Symmetry is handy. We all prefer to be in the galleries that sit between minus one and one, for reasons that are obvious. One tolerates minus-three and plus-three and hopes for the weeks to pass quickly. We spend a week on each level, on a rota of seven weeks. As mentioned, during the day we are each given four posts, each in a different gallery. We may be adjacent to our previous post, or a post we have worked earlier in the day, but we will never be given the same post twice in a day. This is both for respite, which is important, but also to make sure the kind of visitor we face is different. I would suspect it is also to make sure we cannot gain any sort of momentum in working something loose or wearing away any locks. We patrol our galleries for two hours. We are allowed to sit ten minutes. After two hours, we have a fifteen-minute comfort break. After our fourth working hour, we have our lunch hour. After our sixth, another fifteen-minute comfort break. Men and women fought, and if some are to be believed, suffered, for that second break. The Union was big back when the new Museum opened. There is no Union now. After our nine-and-a-half hours, or five-hundred-and-seventieth-minute, the day ends and we return to barracks. Once every seven weeks we are allowed, or rather it is our turn, to take our lunch break in the Clemency Galleries, or Knocking Shops, whatever you'd like to call them, at the back of the Museum.

We stop as we leave the Great Hall and then the Blue team begins to disperse and my stomach knots. I might be food poisoned. The gut is connected to the brain. Odd no one will look at me. Was it the breakfast? I nearly touch Greg's arm.

What are your posts? I ask him.

Thirty-four.

That's the Writing Room. Next to Egypt. It's as far as you can get from Rome in this section.

Fifty-seven. Ninety-one, Greg continues.

Neither of these galleries are in our section.

Mesopotamia. Japan.

Three posts? I ask.

Do you want one? He smiles at me.

What does he mean? Why is everyone leaving for their posts so quickly? Have we definitely been briefed by the curator already? Absent is the two-thousandth-five-hundredth-and-fifty-sixth morning where I stand in a circle and politely chat or stare off in a respectful and ashamed manner.

I'd like to be with my hands in pockets, asking what teammates did the evening before and not listening, knowing what they did in the two hours we have, before we should've gone to sleep. I watch them leave slowly in knitted jumpers, with bulbous arses and straight skinny arms. Never imagining I would miss the awful regularity, I look up to see the curator look down upon our corner, from his staircase nook. The curators, the women and men who had invariably been abroad or in charge, during the problems, have begun to return to the galleries more and more recently. To check not on us, but the objects, or so the optimistic chatter suggests. This curator is not an original curator though. Not even close. He's not an engineer type. Not a designer or architect. They are gone, or really old, gently displaced and replaced by this confident, private class who arefixated on maintenance, not building.

What am I going to do? I mutter to Greg, worried at being watched.

Greg doesn't look at me, to not draw eyes, but passes me a note. How has he got paper? The article is browned and almost cracked. It had print on it, still visible but not readable. It seems to be depicting something beneath the crude felt writing. It is covered in scribbles. Dense scrawls in a hand that is not my own, but similar. In the centre of the handmade bracken, it says *Mark, G22*. As if all that mess were just illustration.

Everything around me feels crude and ridiculous and I wonder why people have always passed notes to me as though I'd just take them. I have always felt at a certain distance, from almost every experience, and maybe that's why. They know I could ball up this rare paper and toss it aside. But that I wouldn't feel strongly enough to do that, they can sense this. I'll take it not because I'm Greg's host, but because I can't imagine the writing contained within will stir me beyond a semi-animal reaction, at best, at worst. Even when I was hands on, strangling.

Even then I was just going with the flow, neither horrified or excited. The aftermath of that, all the classes they sent me to learn about what I had experienced and how I was to feel about it. I just went along with the medicalisation. Took the terminology as symbols rather than profitable analysis. Profit too, I'm just as well with a balance, rather than an advantage. But one must live in hope. Maybe tomorrow I'll be moved to tears.

v

You can touch. You cannot touch. You can have horrible dreams about it all. You can get stabbed in a dark corridor. You can get cut up really badly, without even being stabbed. You can get gored by a hand holding something. Some have even been scalped, in the past. You can have your toes trod on. You can argue this stuff needs to return home, for yourself, and those in earshot, symbolically resisting. You can keep your opinions to yourself. It all doesn't really matter. Either way. You can imagine. You can keep your mind on the task. The museum is a shop for all that. For whatever they like, for whatever we like. It was marvellous really, for a week or so. But over time, you realise. You can realise. No one misses a few visitors. There are so many of them. They float around you like water. Like water you would not drink, even if you had a mouth of sand and pill that cleanses pollution. They are the kind of water that brings with it that which floats. After a time, you think, why bother hurting them? Then you remember.

I carry a small implement. It resembles a gunstock warclub. I got the idea from temporary exhibition. The tool is in a leather sheath, with a one-inch spike and an awkward bevelled head. It'd not be for bringing down on the shoulder, but for picking, caressing, whacking and poking. All those ways can do harm. It could pierce an ear, even. Or puncture a swelling. You have to look after yourself, even when the museum is looking after you. I have never used it. My hands are quite fine. But I have it. And I have showed it. People have thought it an exhibition at my hip even.

To get to Egypt you walk through seven galleries. I pass Augustus, Nero, Caligula, Tiberius, with their children and swimming pools and horrible fake blood. I pass markets with soft manacles for the visitors to try on, in all sizes, small to large. I pass early military tactics, with the shield wall and open toed sandals and the conviction to stab not what is in front of you but what is to your right. I pass gladiators and the trident net combo or the film, with disinfected headphones, on a loop. Some Christian stuff and the automated Seneca. That's just Rome at its quickest, Galleries branch off and on. I pass sea trade, Phoenicians visiting Cornwall for tin, then Mediterranean battles, and some mention then of Abucar and other more modern, though hardly modern, metaphors. Then there's some properly modern paraphernalia, what happened afterwards, how hard an act that was to follow and where it moved onto, the Empire etc...

Some amphitheatre stuff that is so dull it's hard to be still when guarding. Walking through it as the crow flies obviously doesn't present history linearly.

My fellow guards are unpacking their satchels, lifting the seats of their gallery chairs to place things inside. Slowly coming to terms with where they'll be. This is comforting. Still, something in my throat is trying to come up and out, from the stomach. I feel for extra spit with my tongue but it will not come. Through narrow doorways, impractical but based on the old Museum, I keep walking until I reach Gallery twenty-two. My gallery is one long corridor of aged figures, the Coptic Corridor. It has an antechamber with projections, and some mummy coffins they protect with secret devices. The coffins are full, they call them sarcophagi. I find Kevin sat in the chair of the anteroom. He is the most sedate of the team. Lazy, overweight, maybe twice my age or with a really trying habit. He looks at me, barely nods and sits. No curator will bother disturbing him. He's almost certainly been here long enough to be taken for an exhibit. Not a man to toy with mind, as few are.

Alright Kev, I say, and expect no answer.

I begin by checking the space. I am forgetting that I am not Mark. A problem for later?

The fire exit is painted onto the wall, looking real enough, and there are no obvious cracks in the floors, objects or doors. I look down the corridor. The bell rings. Already? Time passes swiftly when I need a moment, and slowly when the opposite is the case. The public have been allowed in. A good minute before they'll make it from The Great Hall to the outer galleries like this. They'll come with shutters clicking, placing themselves in order, rolling in a hampered jog. Why they bother to come and why it keeps them from their homes are not questions with obvious answers. The first ones into every gallery are those who have come specifically for that gallery. I turn and face the statues. Horus, the bird face. Not a word on her beak and yet sound begins in the distance. The crowd are discussing something as they come, I can hear the causing of jams, people flowing around themselves. This is long before I see them. They are eating up the ground of the galleries, moving on, passing over, with others taking their place, beyond corridors, up and down stairs, into the web of adjoining rooms. You think, at this point, they'll get to the end of it. The front line is of a certain kind. Not the stupidest. Quick. They make a silhouette if you watch them come in, like candles stuck into old walls, as though an invisible hand pushed them through in equal space, allowing slips of brightness between their bodies. That is the order of the people, I tend to turn my back first thing, like a good guard. I'm not really noticed by them, after all. By the time I'm surrounded I'm just thinking about how nauseous I am and how I am not really meant to be guarding what I'm guarding.

The first of them to feel moved drops to their knees. Similar melodrama every day. Maybe their grandparents told them they are from the country this object was taken from. When they get a bit tired a few of them will work their way into attacking me for stealing it, as though I did so personally. Motherland myths are part of the reason they pay. So they can have a brief, foreign, satisfactory patriotism in the comfort of a stable place. They almost pray to the things at first, then get crabby as their knees hurt and the reference turns. Same every day. All debris from the place and people they likely hate. They fall for others, to show their children how modest they are. I once believed they would accept their fates with good grace. But then most of the people I met before the Museum didn't have the chance to indulge much. People are gracious at the barrel. And I understand the appalling effect of time must be compensated with some sort of reaction. Time cannot be allowed to remove everything; the mind would break. The kneelers are being helped up. The next thing that happens, every day, is the moment they realise how small they are. The crowds are getting to the Museum's content without conceiving of its true dimensions. Then they start to comprehend just how much there is to look at. Same stages, same faces, same smells.

I check in on Kevin. He's still awake. I patrol. History is such a stupid hobby, I think, as I see their books open, spines broken, looking from picture to thing, thing back to picture. Insipid. I stop by Horus again. A stupid bird-face. Hathor a fat cow-face next to Horus. The other animal heads and the faces. A big waste of clay, or man-hours chopping away, whenever that happened. You can buy tiny Horus' in the shops. Super popular. People love birds. We're not allowed them. A man approaches me with a question. His children are small but it's hard to tell how many he has. His boys have gaunt arms. I can see the smallest child needs the toilet. A toilet question. The other child carries an ice cream. The father has bent the guidebook in his palm. The man leans in close, as they always do. We have training on this, on understanding it. I gravel my teeth while waiting for him to speak. I've got my hand in my pocket of course, always at the ready.

I've a question for you, he says.

What a shock. They so often draw themselves up like this to impress their semi-cognisant issue, growing with every lick of the melting ice cream. It's hot near the wires. The man is going to belittle me at some point. Does he think I'm Mark?

The toilet is down there, I say.

Is it real? He replies, gesturing around us at nothing in particular, not listening.

The second most constant question. He remains unpleasantly close, contented, as though his perceptiveness is a secret he has just revealed, his nose no more than a hands length away from mine. This is it, in a shell; every one of them thinks they are the only one of them despite the immense evidence to the contrary.

I don't know, I have learned to say, to get a bit out but not bite.

So, they're replicas huh? He says and I sense his body being thrown onto a pile.

Oh, I see, I say. No. No. It's all factual.

You change your mind about that, he says.

He's not exceptionally thick then. I'm used to thicker.

What did you say? I ask.

Is it real or not? He repeats, ignoring me, tactically.

What difference does it make? I ask, losing my patience earlier than normal.

What difference? He asks.

It's real. Be done with that, I say. Feasts your eyes. Do what you like.

Can I touch? he replies, taking nothing personally.

No, I say. If you touch, trouble.

My kid wants to touch the baboon, he says jovially, and walks off.

Do that and see what happens, I say after him.

They want to touch as though they were deprived of sight. Touching something supposedly four thousand years old to check if it is. They are fanatical with stirring everything, pretending it's a verification urge. Even though the baboon is obviously older than the child, no matter what its actual origin is. The child's skin is covered in natural oils and dirt and every time he smudges the stone, when my back is turned, it erodes invisible particles, and after years of this, after the weather it might've faced, wherever it was from before we took it, or whenever we made it, it gets malformed and then it has to be carted off and repaired downstairs and all that backache because they insist on grabbing. Not just touching with fingertips, nothing sensual about it, believe me, I've witnessed it thousands of times. It's never a stroke or tickle, a loving trace. It's a slap. A palming. A gripping and feeling and pulping. A testing. The irony is, and I've worked this theory out myself, no one else has had to tell me, this might be the reason they started the big swaps in the first place. Give them what they want. That's not true though. The new Museum was like this from the start. And who knows how the old Museum was? What is there, really, to say it was anything at all? Sometimes I wish simply I could go to the public homes and touch all their belongings. Their houses are probably barren of anything worth touching anyway, apart from small plastic statuettes of Horus.

The children are gone, the heel of the man disappears into the Mummy room after them. The antechamber is not the main Mummy room, of course. That's upstairs, a glamour post. It's a taster in there, Egypt themed. But it's got something to see in it, with the holograms, and Kevin. When I started it was called The Ptolemy Gallery and was all about a well in the Nile Delta. They found something at the bottom of the well. A turtle, I think. It had a bloke wearing a headdress and a serpent. I had to learn to pronounce the word Ptolemaic. Then it was the Goa Stone Gallery. It had just one object, a glass case with a gold ball. In that was a hard glob of something like dirt which the visitors could scrape or dip into a drink they could buy as they walked in. It was a nightmare to work, being a participatory display. There was an incident and they changed it again. This time into the Townley Gallery, whomever they were, some benefactor who scraped their money through some business or another. The Townley had a large green, lidded vessel in the middle of the room. It was engraved. Cista mystica, it was called. That was in lit letters. A 'casket for use in the mysteries' was written below, by hand. All the labels speculated. They said it was a big import-ant box in the ancient cults of the god Dionysus. But we made it full of old biscuit paper and lost property scraps in the modern cult of the Museum guards. That was the joke, and the curators never lifted the lid, or didn't care. That was where I put all my

cups, in the mysterical box. That ended last year. It seems
smaller now, less fun, with the little Mummies being more of
a draw.

With nothing else to do I follow the man and his family
to the edge of the doorway between my corridor and this chamber, seeing what I think is the mother trailing by. They are trying
to escape me after all, obviously onwards to tickle and touch.
Kevin'll see them. He is not to be underestimated. Whether he'll
intervene or not will depend on his mood, and that's up to him,
fine by me either way. A gamble the family will not know they're
making. Just as they won't know some of the objects have minor
electric blockades. I glance down the corridor, checking to see
whether there is anything seeing me. I won't be caught off post.
Today of all days. At some point I need to speak to someone
about not being Mark. It's always the ways with these constant,
menial jobs. When something goes wrong, no one cares.
When you are being someone you are not, pretending to be
Mark, they don't even notice. But when you are you, where you
should be, you can be reprimanded at any minute. For now,
technically my responsibility ends at the line between the
Coptic Corridor and the little Mummies, no matter who I am.
Before I can even reach the line dividing the corridor from the
antechamber, I hear a buzzing and I smell its work. Then I hear
Kevin bark. It's a single hoot. He's laughed. I wonder if it's hit
the children.

The father, who has hauled behind him his offspring,
restraining them, as though they were just a cluster of splashes,
has returned to me, the hair on his right arm cooked like pig
skin. Predictably, he seeks to engage in the typical embar-
rassed-aggressive confrontation, testing other defences in yet
another customary act of visitor futility. I point to one of
mummies in the box behind him, a small one, leaning into
to the antechamber but keeping my feet behind the line.

That person was killed because they were rude, I say.
Have a quick think about that.

I lift my hand from my pocket and work it firmly into a
fist and then I palm my gunstock warclub with a smooth motion.
I return it to its pocket, to not attract attention from nosy and
uninvolved visitors. I want him to decide and I see the decisions
pass over his face as he sails right by me. I give Kev the thumbs
up. I watch the man drag his kids further down the Coptic
corridor.

Naturally, I follow him. Something to do. Swiping through the crowd, who stumble and bank at his passing, I move in his wake. I make it halfway down the corridor, well after the family, and am met by the sight of the father with both of his hands upon the face of a statue. Anubis, the jackal. My favourite. The only one who doesn't look like an idiot. How would he know? His children, like him, have their hands splayed open, palms of their thumbs touching, forming a fan of fingers and sweating, pressing skin. His wife just watches. The man has his hands over the dog-headed god's cheeks, his thumbs resting just below the eyes, which are white stone pebbles in an otherwise nocturnal black basalt. Anubis does not regard them, squatted on a stone bench, eyes above. They cannot reach his eyeline, even when he is on his haunches, eternally. It appears as if Anubis will not deign to answer the servant's question. The ends of his extensive canine jaw are worn into a pout that seems supercilious, and brilliant. I cannot believe Anubis is a downstairs job. He may be real, and only us who see it often will notice. The man and his boys do not see it. They are square on with him, eye to eye, not recognising his vision is three hundred and sixty degrees, set into the side of his head. Nor does their mother, stood away, unhappily posing them for photographs, lackadaisically imploring them to crane their necks while their hands are sowed into the stone. The picture will show the boy's hands cover the instep of Anubis' feet, or claws, or paws, as you wished. It will show their father lathering his face. This seems significant. They think he's made of soap.

I take a moment to survey the scene. To observe potential witnesses. This is stimulating. This is why I got into this line of work. Action, without the relentless campaigning. This is more than the normal morning. This could now be a minor incident. It might even bring attention to my not being where I should be. I have reasons to interject suitably. Even the visitors know this is the new Museum, where you can't needle a guard and expect nothing. They may argue, as all do, that they were not provoking me, and that my feelings are incidental. Either way, just as I have no one to report my confusions to, so the visitors have no one to complain to. There is no self-broadcasting now, to protect them from themselves. In this regard the world has turned twice over. Like it says in the Spangler Gallery, everything has changed since we were children. Everyone cannot do everything and be miserable. Everyone

can only do what they can do, and be content at that, as we
have learned.

I reach the trio and sweep the man's hands away in one
forceless motion. He falls, and his hands land loudly on the
ceramic floor, stopping his face. His hand was so open it doesn't
close, and breaks his fall. Must've slapped though, like a stiff
body falling into water. No other visitors want to look like they
notice. The man is alone, and even his children step away. I
often say the public don't notice me, but they know who I am in
the Galleries. That's why, deep down, I like it when they touch.
We all have a dark heart. The man is crouched, I grab his collar
and drag him into himself, bending him, my legs stepped deep
into a squat beside his back. He tumbles and bumps into the
boys and like a collapsing building they collide with each other
and onto their father. The man tries to stop splaying, taking
great handfuls of his children as he does. There is no expression
of anger on his face. No report is coming. However, his mouth is
opening, and he is beginning to speak as I reach down to take a
handful of his hair, to pull him back to his feet, where I suppose,
I might drive his face into Anubis'. To show him which will re-
lent first, the old stone or the new visitor. I might not though.
I think I'll find out at the top. As I reach down, I feel a touch
upon my bicep and am instantly relieved. I turn to face the
curator who looks down at me, his hand passive in its control
upon my arm, his face perfectly gentle. He is betrayed by an
almost importable dampness.

You must not touch them, he says disdainfully, and nods
at the floored man.

I am sorry, I reply, unsurprised.

They get alarmed, he reasonably insists, leaning in.

The father, still not fully righted, is helped up by his wife
and they all hasten on, making the end of the Coptic corridor,
half crawling, simmering into the masses who do not want to
know. They rush down the first few drops of the north stairs, out
towards Asia, likely to touch the treasures there, when suitably
recovered. There are new rules on the new levels, some things
can be fondled. The thought of their grubbing flashes across
my mind. That, with the general feeling of discontent and nausea, becomes a disregard that makes me temporarily forgetful
of the silent wonder expected toward a curator. I speak again,
maintaining a tone of mediation while doing something I
have never seen anyone do before.

If I cannot touch them, how are we to stop them touching?

I have always wanted to ask that question. The curator breaks contact with me. If it were possible, he'd look downcast, as though he were now facilitating words between Dogface and I, like Anubis had interjected on my behalf. Or as if he didn't know the answer. Anubis would remind his living keeper that without the threat of Guards like me, in a Museum of tackles and pins, then no one could be expected to follow any rules. I feel creeped and try not to stare. They look similar, this curator and the doglord. The man too has a protuberance of a face, coming up over his collar, with big teeth, and clean, hairless cheeks. He is as much a polished lump of brass as his accent.

You must just keep asking them not to, he tells me.

But this stuff is important, I say, and gesture to Anubis again.

The curator seems to dig in and flee himself in the same moment. He holds his own hand up to his own chin, and there is such a lot of sweat above it, on his forehead, that it seems he's sicker than I. He's young. It seems a terrible time to tell him I'm not Mark and I need my real posts and I don't feel well, but I am reminded of all those things by his perspiration. I choose not to, and he beckons me towards him once again. This is one human face I am willing to be closer to, for the novelty, if nothing else.

It's all not real, he intones.

It's not all real? I ask, equally quiet.

It's all not real, he repeats, a little louder.

We both look down the corridor, not knowing where else to look, which is normal for the Museum. Down the lines again, of busts and statues, gods and animals, all made up and fantastic, bits and bobs creased and jotted about, as though they were frozen in a moment, their bodies missing and broken on purpose, some of them simply a head, then a giant foot, then a baboon, then a sphinx. Whatever it is its altogether around us and like logs in a river, it's still points between an ever moving populous. We look at the Egyptian gods, he looks, then I. Their alignment awkward, so that they are a perfect row of old faces. The falcon, the turtle, the jackal, the crocodile. Something for the public to relate to. This moment the curator and I share, it feels I am not the only one to see them as confusions.

I..., I said.

While they are contravening you, the curator interrupts, to caress these things, he gestures to Anubis, they are... hectic. That is the best we can ask for.

But...

It is true, it is not working like it used to. He sighs as he says.

That's okay, I say, and feel embarrassed for being too nice.

Please, he says, and I interrupt.

But Anubis. He's real right?

Please, he replies, just keep telling them. Not to touch.

I'm not busy, I reply, feeling sorry for myself, and my temporary god as good as any in the shape of a pet I once had, out in the field. I look at the feet of the dog headed big boy and say, I'm always happy to intervene, I've nothing else to do.

The curator sighs again, as though relieved, and it seems as though he touches my shoulder in relief, but this cannot be the case. I won't check. I will not be led by an urge to verify. The uniforms are quite thick.

The urge they have to test, he goes on, unnecessarily, whether it's genuine, this is the least of it, he says, appearing to now speak to himself alone.

The least of it? I ask, extending our conversation because I don't want him to feel guilty, or pointless.

They just need to be left alone in that. They are not trying to know if it's real or not, you follow? They are trying not to know. The opposite. Do you understand?

No, I say. I do not understand.

For the act itself, to feel they can, he says.

I understand, I reply.

Good. We are talking, he says.

Yes. This is a new conversation, I say. A conversation.

Yes, it is. Though some of us are having different ones at once, he says, pointing around us, at the public, and the exhibits, and not Anubis or I.

Then the curator seems to slump, and would sag if he were not stood upright.

If they can be told not to touch, we can stay here? I ask to affirm.

Yes. That's right. You've got it.

Okay, I reaffirm.

The curator seems to grow again. He bulges to leave but then doesn't. He hovers, unthreateningly, intimidating me.

The objects are real, of course. I mean, what I said

before, it's the whole actual thing that isn't, he says.

I nod.

The building is made of paper, he says. At some level, the floors are plastic. The signage is mache. The food is mush. The water is gas. The trees outside, they are plastic.

A frog in my throat, I realise he is mad. At this, the curator wanders off, his back to me, shaped in tweed.

Bloody hell, I whisper.

I hear him speak before I see him turn to me.

Thanks Mark, he says.

Off he strides and I watch him go. Before he reaches the end of the corridor, where they all go eventually, I hear him say, to an asking visitor, that the toilet is *la bas*. As though self-conscious, he has forgotten he need not spontaneously offer directions to the bathroom, as that is my job, or the job of the visitor host. The asking visitor looks like they really need to go and there is nearly empathy in the posture of the curator.

Have a fine day, I shout down the hall after him.

You are doing a good job.

The curator does not acknowledge my encouragement and leaves once and for all. I look back once more at Anubis and am reminded of Kevin, and for some reason his younger iteration, Greg. I really see how ridiculous it is to have a man with a dog's head exhibited for every man, woman and child to stare at as though that meant something. Imagine the ideas this abomination provokes. And even stupider for it to be put in the middle of a gallery. Just like that. Just because it is said to be from the past. An answer to a question no one would've asked. I pat down the doghead and run my index finger down the line of his gums before I wander back down the corridor towards the Sphinx.

VI

Kevin relieves me before my replacement arrives. Often, we create these moments of release. We are impatient to move when moving is near. Kevin does this as it's tradition, he isn't being nice. On my way to the canteen, back down the Coptic corridor again, eyes averted as I pass the big dog, and twisting towards the door that appears a cupboard, beyond which it is *Staff Only*, I encounter a small prostrate body lying in a walkway. Visitors swarm by, like water around an island. A few colleagues I don't know, guards and hosts both, crouch over the child. The child is babbling about something. He is remembering his memories. He keeps saying *I remember* and *My dad*. His head a bit split open. They wait for a first-aider to respond on the radio. No one has so far. They wait. Just in case the child is really hurt, and they make a mistake tending the wound. My colleagues are bound to do nothing. The child is grabbing a colleagues' arm, talking to him, so the man has to look down, at them. It's Albert from the Silver team. I had only not recognised him from the back of his head. I hear the word *quiet*. On a normal day I would not get involved.

I walk towards them and Albert sees me, stands and leaves. He sees me but he does not look at me. What did I do? How many of us have wondered this and attributed the behaviour of others to ourselves? The host, whom I don't know front and back, approaches me. I'm solid and don't flee like Albert. Cynthia, she says. If you're here, she adds, and walks off too, towards the cupboard that leads to the canteen. The child is a boy. He must've fallen over, striking his head on a bust. His family are not around. He had run away? Has Albert called for a cleaner, as well as a medic? A cleaner to clean the blood from the column supporting the bust as well as the floor. The boy is mumbling, again about his father, something more he's remembering. Did his father warn him not to run in the Museum? Did his father cause his headwound? I lean down and touch his shoulder. I can see he can no longer feels the scalp wound. But my, how scalps bleed.

Don't worry, I say, you aren't in trouble for crying.

There continues to be a slight leak of new blood, though it's coagulating nicely, and I feel a flash of nostalgia. At times the boy can't catch his breath. If I had no experience with wounds, I'd think this serious. But it's not. The scalp bleeds like nothing else, they are dramatic caps upon our skulls. The boy continues to calm, and lies like a quadruped sleeping, fingers touching toes as though his limbs were bound and his mouth partially open. Like a fallen horse. He rolls a bit, on his back to his side. I hear a shout from behind me. I stand and leave and do not look back. I assume it's his dad who has finally found him.

In the canteen, the hosts sit huddled, closely knit, while guards are saying little in more scattered groups. Canteen workers say even less. In fragments of sentences there are orders, for tea, other black drinks, lots of water. Anything that will require a toilet break or two from the upcoming post. Some are coldly expressing something against someone not present. Others stare out, time ebbing away, perhaps then a chat about what I cannot imagine. Amongst them, I see Greg, his back straight. I feel an urge to avoid him. Beyond that, in this moment, I'd like to never speak with him again. I nod at him, but I do not think he sees me, as he does not return the acknowledgement. Miffed, I sit away from others as I had hoped to anyway.

The canteen hall is the most standard gallery. Everything is legible and not overtly emblematic. Just dead furniture, plastic and grey blue. Like a hospital waiting room. I have been in places like this since I was a teenager, resting. The various units of people, how they sit around me, plotting in their own way. It forces a memory upon me. I am tired too, as I was then. I have a good thing to recall, a harder time but with more intent. It is not a dream I am thinking of. How do memories begin? Dinner was served. We gathered once at a table in a large tent, in the dim of a single flare. We ate curdled milk and potatoes and the tent smelled of unwashed workers. Me being one of them. Things were tense because everyone was tough as shit, but we got on with it. The canteen mother grazed the ring of us. We were hers. She was old. We gave her the food and she made it. A napkin was placed in my palm. I had one hand free to carry the tray. I was serving, younger than the others, but not a waiter. I was doing my bit, and soon, I was sat around, eating, older. I saw bloated faces squinting up into a plate. Like a well with a body in it. Something you see from far above and think, that really looks like something it can't be. Just like here in Museum. It seems I was cut out to see impossible things. There was a silence throughout the tent because we'd been clearing houses that day. More than usual. Not one or two, but a whole row of houses. A silence that amplified nothing. What was being ruined beyond us wasn't there. The meek conversations had come to an end in the huddle, and sitting motionless, my comrades watched a moth bumping into a glass that was reflecting the flare light. In a corner of the tent a man was taking a gun to pieces and trying to repair it. He cleaned it first, with the under tails of his shirt. I saw the sudden movement of his jaw, suddenly biting into a thread of something food-like. Then the gun was rebuilt, stitched like teeth through an unchewable object. I had real focus then, just earth vision. I was so perceptive. I saw no one else flinch, no one else notice what the man was chewing. I saw no one else move to the corners of the tent with their eyes. But then I saw what was actually between his teeth. There was plenty of food, but he was just in the habit. I loved that time. I could do whatever I liked.

I can smell bad tea and a host, one table away from me, seems to put her blouse aside. She lifts the shirt off her head. She leans her arm out of uniform, over herself. The sliver of her arm shows bright skin. She makes me self-aware. There is nothing inappropriate or notable about this, but I can smell body odour. It's oddly pleasing, but such a different kind of smell. The deodorant that is battling to cover it, it makes the tent disappear. Then I see a glimpse of a hidden temp uniform beneath her dress code sweater. Strange. And there is Rebecca, I see her behind this host. She is talking to Greg. She is lightly sweating or freshly showered or just reflecting light. She looks to be in a foul mood, still. I wonder if she's old enough to have been in a tent? Could be why she's so angry with me all the time. Is it hot for other people? She appears serene, until a word from Greg seems to alarm her. She passes her fingers over her own hands as though she hates me. She is rubbing some sort of lotion, she smells her fingers, as one would a flower. I see a change in Greg's face too. His tenderness seems evaporated, among the halogen lights. He is telling her something with and in confidence. Are they suddenly united on a task against me? They know why I've not been given my posts I think. Greg, usually so stone-ish, leans his arm over her, brushes her hair behind her ear like a lover and whispers something even less intimate. I am both surprised and relieved. At least the unfamiliar is constant. We aren't allowed to touch in public. Greg has won me over to the facts of abnormality today. What follows is so simple and easy, the word yes, her mouth, stressed. Greg stands, looks directly at me, and waves me over. I look back and sit still. I check the clock. Ten of my fifteen minutes are gone. His face remains implacable. I realise I remembered the tent because it ended on a moment like this, where all around can be felt the end of something. Who is Greg to wave me? I fondle the tiny wooden club on my belt and think how much it looks like a pipe. I then stand and walk directly towards Greg and Rebecca.

What? I ask Greg? Which galleries are you returning to? I ask Rebecca.

Medieval, Rebecca says, curtly.

Sit with us, says Greg.

Say please, I say, and sit.

Then Greg looks past my shoulder, at something further down the corridor that leads back to the galleries. Staring into space, his face that of a statue, a bird.

Have a drink, he says.

You first, I reply.

Greg pushes over to me his tea and I drink it because I am thinking of what is happening and what he is looking at. My retort was instinctual. I do not look down at the drink though I can imprecisely smell it is not good tea but something else, and I think it's the memory of that woman host's body odour. On the tongue it is like water but thicker. Not so bad. Weak tea. I have drank the drink Greg has given me, and despite its darkening odour, now getting deeper into the body, I drink it again. Why do I feel the need to prove something to these people? Out there, I would've laced them. The liquid milks as I finally look down upon it and fogs further as I neck the dregs. Perhaps now there will be an obvious reason why I feel funny. And no one can say I backed down. But I feel nothing. When it wears off later, I'll forget, so I'd better mention this now, before I won't know.

Thanks a tonne, I say.

My friend my friend my friend, he replies.

Greg has never spoken to me like that before. He reaches out, holds my arm by the bicep, and I stand and then, happily, he leads me by the arm. Something else he has never done before.

How about a walk? I'll walk you to your next post if you like? He asks.

Oh?

The Writing Room. I am sure it is in good hands until we arrive.

We?

You.

Of course, I reply.

I have stopped knowing fully where or when we are and follow him. We walk towards the library, the Writing Room. We walk as though we have just met. Ceremoniously. I suspect he has taken some decision. Greg still stands at my arm. His proximity is cynical. We pass the corridor; the small boy is gone. Greg almost holds me. We pass through The Great Hall. I do not know the turn we have taken. We pass the door to the library. Rebecca is with us for this journey. We are taking her first to the Medieval gallery, straight across the Museum. The rooms are filled with rays and shadows like a candlelit dinner, blazing lamps bristling like trees on fire. We scoot happily through. We are then walking towards a guard on duty and she looks up at us, unsurprised. She is still sitting on her chair as we reach her, something clasped, hidden in her hand, now passed to Greg.

Are we disturbing you? Greg asks.

Not at all, she replies.

I am just going to walk to the Writing Room, he says.

Is that your gallery, she asks?

No, it is his, Greg says.

Do you need to get back to yours? she asks.

No, he says. I have arranged for cover.

Are they robots? She stands up, and unwraps her jumper. It was tied round her neck. Why can't I place her name? What team is she on? Rebecca watches her eagerness, which may have only been politeness, as if to learn how to operate at work. I sense an element of such shamelessness that I can't help thinking they are all having an affair, and why keep it from me? Why show it to me at all? Have I communicated somehow that I care about such things? Such natural, if unexpected, relationships people timid, sheltered, boring people. Colleagues and co-workers. But then, is it that I can only think in terms of sex when it comes to strange behaviour in colleagues of the same? Precisely because, compared to me, they are so pacific? Why is everything moving with me, and not against, as usual?

Greg lifts my arm again. He keeps touching me. I'd snatch him up if I felt like it. Together we hug walls, keeping off from the visitors, walking across the gallery. Rebecca is still with us. Like a guard of the guards. A job good for charitable Rebecca, whom I know intimately, as I'm sure everyone has guessed.

Are you going to the training with him? She asks Greg.

No, he replies. He's rota'd for the Relief at lunch.

He is referring to the shop. The concession gallery and

I think, oh yeah? She smiles at me and I see the female guard is gone and Rebecca is sat in her place, and we are leaving her to it. She's smiling goodbye.

Greg is staring at our reflection in the cases as we go. I see us and I see objects. I repeat the word. Weapons, and a sub-heading sticks in the mind. *Trauma and cleaving weapons.* It's on a label. I try faintly to reach out and grab. The battle axe, the Bec de Corbin, the bludgeon and club. The flail and flanged mace. The horseman's pick and the morning star. I see a skinny man carved into wood. And books. Medieval themed. I want to read them. But Greg leads me on. His is the outer track. He doesn't bump into anyone. It seems more than I Greg knows every corridor, every path, lane, garden, hidden lightswitch and cupboard, every gallery, even. A woman attempt to stop us, and ask where the toilet is. He does not reply to her, and this refusal to answer the simple question, which leaves her quietly wandering away, is curious. Another guard is approaching her, whomever is working the gallery we are passing, between Medieval and The Writing Room. Again, I don't really know them, the guard from another team. A temp. Again. He is young, he is not looking at us, he is having a leisurely chat with the visitor, who is like a labourer leaning negligently against a machine, a case that towers above, supporting the roof of the gallery. A glass column. The back of the temp's head looks like the back of Mark's head. Ratty blonde. But this isn't Mark. I am unable to hear his words, but see a big smile upon the face of the visitor.

Well, that was rude, I say.

Greg leads me on, around the edges of this gallery. How late I am to the galleries not yet given to me. I am not a visitor, I can't own anything, nothing can belong to me. Greg and Rebecca seem to know. I seem compelled.

Now I am sitting. What a relief. I am responsible for their meeting, Greg and Rebecca, and now he needs me out of the way. I hope so. My god, I forgot how fine The Writing Room is.

VII

Since Iave workd at the Mueum I have wrotten 486 notes. I've
sen people drawing freehan maps of acuracy been talked to like
they're paeces of wortless dogsht and this's why I don draw. Ive
seen shutters shutterd like winows in the face of so many wokers
that all blinds have drawn into aan eclipse. I have witnessed
rosella stone backpacks, launchboxes of the greatwave, posters
of pandora's box. Ive seen prayer rug mousemats. Ive been a
witness of commercial objectts. I have ben bystander to drink
at cafés that's everything. Sometimes I don feel weel working.
This is the right way to give a version, in the corner of the boks,
where M is Muster, the passing od, the readings room. In a
notebok Ihav lists of peole whoere colleages. They are moved
because the rise of the provisioal, the Simos, and Ive avowd
myself not to those who are traped in complan. Sweep of the
yung, like pograms, for not much, for it is boring woking.
I don know what.
 I have to check the roum for obstacles. My head achs. I am
clearing a bit beter now. I sat. As times are passing always slowly
in the reeding roum. I see if balcony, and desks, and boks, are
still ther. Soon. Sittung in a roum, alon, is not wok. I'm patetic.
How is doing nuthing ajob? I sitt longer.
 In the endles dead hours of a dead wok the sevens go toth
tens, the fives to sevns, and you fin chasing womn physically
to expres to them aganst yurself a desire to not only be bored
but to be with them, when you are not aloud to be so. I shak my
heed. The ones in charge, honsty, are the one who wil sack the
girls if they don at least smil. Not lik Rebecc. A killer. But am I,
was I, a refug or just blind that I amaother of those unwelcom
faces wen some person is jus trying to jst make their way? A
witnes. To Rebeca. I don evn li kheer.

My record is free in a day. A hoast, a gard and a vistor. Tempring, meen to kind, why wuld anyon let me? But always opin pursd to me? Friens. Shadows in ancase. Even if the morasses of the facleses are not louking into that cases, for an objett they've nevir huard of anll never remeber! I canot hid beneth heed's hair. Womn who are the rivals of Mueums? Mueums. Musems. Musums. Meseums. I coup my ears to the big doome above me. I from what they're hiding. Wok. But newe twins to my being so boredd her and them being singled an arived from the surg. Thessaloniky, Tallynn, Milann, Bocharest, Wroclaw and Wilnius. Never to forgette, thick, not tiick, all it is te sam. One telling meon in the end they knoiws, eves as heavy lip, the way of the buoble, poping a joint, under the crusx of an omoplata. An ippon seoinage. Joudo learnt in war, that nearly broke a neck in gallery 1! In a diffrent disaled toilet in the chilen's centr. Tha was the third on sight, the third in a day. Plaing the plasteer beed game on my lunch with a ballpoin pen and the gorl from canten. Lingring, like silvefish, caugh short, more like a whet patch in bathrom, held tiht like a tortise. Like tunks of titt. Then a swift bip back on to the gallery, and raist peeple can change, the old sins, signse, says, in the nostala galleies, and thene while she, Augstus' first wif, kills baies for the orb, I'm scrathing trousr crotch patach before Haedrian in sevent. O Ana O, in the numer zero. Foshmouth when she's hading blindnes.

Every womn dies alone her, she said. I tred to lok away, pretend
I'm don. I'm the Chris who ponds the dessert. I saw him just
a bit ago, in the Medioval. Our old pall, savfiour. Before we hav
thes jobs to doe. The salt of the salt moth Jesus, who forgives
the visior who know so moch they stos to tell me withan a polite
converation. Will my maid be plucked in heavn? or Virtuos?
I'd prefer to clen, if the help aren't slot for time and are shot
for the machine gan on the crow's nest. I had one. It's like, surrounded by all these books, and no one loking abound for them,
I'm wake frum nightmares all the same, with an erection, next
to me, going limp, falling sleep gain. Itws fine, happens.
Mark was sayin that.

mment begins with no visiors. Iave to start to wnder
ng Room are open to the publi? For which I shuld
ful.

..lere are two cases to the Mongolles, one to Timure the
Lame. Do hey know were they wend? M gallery is where. M
is moar, the trumpts or sunding. I cain do it fur them, sifted
thrugh thousands upon people to afform the levitating feling
of exciting lov that floots abuve us abuve us with jus a few, anis
only possible despit the appearance of emptines from mass.
I have discovred actually it is possible only in the moss. It is
a flood prophecesed. The first of the Mueum womn I trough,
the hidden dour of the enlightanmen gallees, from Lusitania,
and the Monguls were the biggest gentic studies revels the
one singul DNA strainin thousads was Cingiz humself. Maibe
apoucraphyl, but one gorl I visitd, she has definely rouded ees.
I'm feeling a bit aruused. It was her, not having reed the books
on mogolls that I've red who point that they easily reeched
the bailtic beaes. Hare was vikingy, and her ees nut. Whiches
stiring in a dark roum on the minute break frum a shaft in the
enlightanment ery. The dour opens with a Hous key, ate lorridor
goes nowoere, a remnance of sume past developmants, some
labe. Offe into the eest roods, where the post offise wishes it is.
Maibe once undergrund when they had to plan to evauate the
objetts out of the mueum in a hurry because new boms. Museun.
Mueum. Just feets from or flouring the roug columns of the nel-
ightanman still the shrappnel of thoe old boms that tore trough
the roof of lostmakers. Fore this a placements of losts, lists,
is what Mueum is. Just feat I held her aroond a waist. It was like
a show I wasin, an exhibiting myself.

Strange the reading room isn't being bread today. No visiors
at al. I will gett on and realy check the balcony, bok, desk now.
In a minut, when my hed clears. I'm nut doroling.

The nitemar is the excess of Mueum is it's imossible. If
grosly founded bloated grey room and in each a single objett,
the cyruss cyliner, the beginning luws, the floud tablets, the
ramm in the ticket, the better before us, any of them, they'd
respect it. The dead bodies, are they actually dead we asked?
Wat I need focus. The were-men, womn and now they are rased
husk, the horrus, the legs up, the brests harpies, the gainte black
stone beetle the size of a man curling to protect from blouws.
I can remember most objets, if I try. I'm sat up in reading roum.
How marvel to doing this. The gatres of beerds of bulls of the
burn, the stanes of sold where shiep were grasing. The revisions
without chains, or claps, or even weapuns really, maybe a
samura sord, maybe a case in the chinse gallery worth beyond
measures. The Jade bok. The Jade Terapin. The ring and sword
of Tiupu sultan. It's fortunate, the feejee mermaid, that the
historie of people is swallowed up, in the new neded pylation.
Because if they knew wat we haddone they wuld swell so lurge
to broke the seems of any build, let alone a Mueum! But these
are sid by sid. By the thousand, how can they posibility take it
on? How can these objetts be reel, when nombers are amassed
as thogh they were visiors themselves. The behind glass're
expanding with the resuls of medicane that is decried still by
people who believe in a goad when in the Mueum you can trace
where other ons ended? I've reed in these boks, they would have
special turns in the Mueum, the first Musuem. Funshows. Come
and unwrop a mummi was one. They could pay and peal off the
rottn sand bandagys of a prole of the time, nothing important
like someone peeling. Then they rediscoved Troye, or the Ashiria
gates, and that was a senaton. How did they move such large
objetts? The dicks are hackd off because of Mueum, the olde
Musuem, the on before, and cause, like fingrs, they are vulnerabl
when moved. They teld me. The is in room four, in the centre.
I have never heard of that objett, you must have dreemt it,
I sayd. The coiled serpet was given by Motesuma to Cort, to a
king, and then pope, an bought by a private deal. But walls has
a beam alarm, and if children pass hands through the beem the
alorm sounds, insted. The old history says Cooke expeditions
brought back with it, or Calvaries, or Claudio Rich, or the work
of Lunnaeus.

Iave come part of the organisatin I kind of didn defere,
of record into times, that needs by is first, only end anorder. The
beginning of anorder, the age of needling to record things, in
anorder to give an accounts, of things, as then might have been.
Which changes how they are. Do I like an enginer, I wear a radio.
Is not making nose today. Liss of those to be departd, lists of
those to be refusd, entry, or exit. Lists of these whos culture con-
fused them when it comes to the reed cord dangling in a disaled
toilet. It is an alarm. Not a flush. Five letters. M U E U M, six, five,
for those playig who poor through the other singin alarming fire
exists as though they're ways out. There are only two ways out,
as evr, mouth and backdoor.

I again have to check the roum for obstacles. My head
achs mor. I am clearing colours a bit beter now I sat as times are
passing. I look upon the lip to see the gardenr himself is soon
too much. That ain't Mark and it ain't curator again. My hed
has always been strung at clearing. If they are going to hurt me
like this I'll be leaving here within a yer by design. All fine in t
he Reeding Room. Rightin. The balcony has a railing. I huld it,
my hed. I see down on the empty desks and focos.

A healthy hert beats my chest. Trees plucked clean up in
ninety-four by the sprang, by the Primae Noctis, by a cry of birth.
The detetive one misery lets go like fingers uncurling from a
branch. The dream in room four; a woe'd beggard approaches
gastric, palsy overload. Someone I hart or a coleag? He asks for
me. Is he asking for? Or me sun, for now. Dogfights, breathing
heavy to remain in life for soon enough anyhow. E is for empty, O
is for I. The song of colleags saying nasty things behind yor back
in the workplace. A big poddle in the gallery for here it is always
raining. Shades of green to yellow, blue, purple, pink and finally
back to its original green. It is as tough the water freezes evenly.
But this is in simple language. Sit ready, get paid for thats, in a
chair, in an all but empty room. Give up smoking, alcohol. Do
not touch, and if you cannot sit alone with yourself. The silent
instructions—readiness, the single driptime to feel one's health
from the innards and give thanks for menial labour, the teacher
with a voice. Slow at wanting fast, fast at wanting slow. Dribbling
into the perception of each minute. Not the worst I've done,
breaking wind in children's faces, telling them so, and forward
rolls in the war gallery, where my fighting comes in handy.
The sound of a bike chain, locking as disease falls, as children
are torn from their parents, as mercy looms what boredom has

taught me, this is a human recourse, there are pits to dig, a
bored. A list of; a sadness addresses. Thick varicosal veins says
one and wonder why, in the long of the blue flower there is no
mention it will soon be gone. The pantheon of western diseases
abound—fatigue, arrhythmia, angina … cancer. A desire to
charge one's phone before the stone. The false attachment to
the body—a radio that rots waves. A really bad diet, for the
usual up the left shoulder by pickpockets in their thieves again.
Mental is our new canteen but salute to the worker, they are the
soil in which hope is grown, wait for a minute… violins, a march,
it's a year, the urn is strong. I smell petrol, and finally after
so many thousand false starts this abandoned bag turns out
to a premonition.

   I'll look about but stay put. If I get caught off post, I will
become 'suspended.' Mark is gone, I realise. They have planned
nothing. There is a roof in here. Desks. Books. Nothing else.
Wood, yes. And my eyes fixed on going home, and out of the
building, where there is no more building. No homes there and
little in the way of kindness. Just huddled together for warmth.
I need to watch my gallery; I am the u in undergrowth. It is the
library, where most of the body is on course: Undertheground.
The girls was in the reading room a few times now that I remember. I'll sit again. Lots of spit coming out. Meanwhile I know
where above I am standing on and that you can never see again
and I have never seen. Over the desks of the reading room, far
below the dome, there lies a covering floor on which the statues
stand, deading. It's a dead temple. But I know about it, I have
spent an at least two hundred, maybe up to five hundred hours
in that dome. I know the writers who were here. Russle, Shawe,
Beck, Poune, Strain, James, Orell, Kipple, Stokes, Wild, Huley,
George, Thomas, Frost, Galswill, Hard and Lenny. And Trotty.
But did any of them have sex there? Any of them checking fire
exits, finding themselves amidst the desks, underneath the
stilted over propped up cover of those desks to hold above it
an exhibition for paying public? Taking it down there and lift
up onto one of those desks and pull onto the floor and where
they were something they never could do? Because it would've
been remembered. I remember, and I have been there, and that
is the right of one who has worked among the watch, taking it
in so they can go back. Because what is worth doing in the now
writiing room is best now seen by an audience but wiped out
with a wet tissue before the next break comes along. Of course

there is no trace of those names, there is only their books at all. Because the books in the library Mueum no longer are with the material there, just the knowledge they were there. I wiped semen off the floor of the writing room with my sole of the shoe. Was it mine? One of the other names I knew before, which I knew had been off the top of my head as I wrote this and didn't have to look it up at what is beneath me as I sit on my arse.

The Dome is surrounded by The Great Hall. Beneath the white empty court there are many levels into the basement. Other soldiers once did my job. There is a shooting range beneath the court appropriately deep levels down, and there was a station too. There was a suicide in the court once, near when I started. A man jumped and deliberately went head first. He took a few days to die, which I can't imagine was the case. But it happened before I worked at the Mueum. They did shut the Mueum that day, but not on the bombings. Just before me too. I didn't have anything to do with that.

There are cabinets in the Egyptian basement like those of the libarry, but ten feet tall at least, that are wheeled open with black levers. They are filed rows of dead human bodies, their moisture departed. That room smells not of rot but of something far worse. You know when it's been opened. It must be lunch soon. Back out of the quiet domes and into a surge. I've gone from aroused to lonely. It must be lunch soon.

VIII

I am conscious. Being showered, shaved, perfumed and talced.
I'm dressed in clean underwear. I am wearing work shoes, black
imitation leather, but not my own shoes. I descend some stairs
and must return for a coat. I feel unnaturally clean, very English,
as if I have no reason to be. I am self-conscious, smelling so
strongly, aware of myself and my own thoughts, scrubbed fresh
like some ghost. I am trying to revel in the humour of washing.
I have a horrible headache which suggests I've agreed to these
experiments, and not for the first time. I imprecisely remember
some books and a presentiment and the absence of a dream,
for they aren't actual, and no one wants to hear about my dreams.
I feel sexual and abstracted, but physical, prepared. What feels
unusual is that when I am relieved from the Writing Room,
my colleague is completely alone. That is, once they set me on
my way, I feel it is just them doing so.

I'm on an upper landing. It's a long passage with some
doors like the fronts of small houses. As if I were on the outside
and each door would indicate multiple dwellings, and the com-
munity of different kinds of people. I am alert, inside a place,
outside my mind, as though I'm in a cave. I haven't been on a
street for seven years. It doesn't seem important. I am my own
innocuity. No one cares to see me see them. A cleaner is in the
hallway with me, and she glares at me. I'm not all alone. She
stops her sweeping, rests her arm on her broom. Her phospho-
rescent uniform is green and olive. This is the kind who will
have been on the ghost before me, cleaning up after the last
whose turn came. It is an expensive looking door I stop before.
My eyes itch. I walk past the door at first, aware that it's a desti-
nation. The grubby paper in my hand says seven and the door
has a number upon it. I walk by. I loiter until the cleaner leaves,
or I can't see them, and try to ignore my impeded eyesight. I rub
my eyes, they water and turn red. I must wait until the cleaner
has cleared off or I will look like I have been taking drugs. This
matters to me. The cleaner will have better things to clean than
floors outside a bagnio. There are objects getting dust.

Above an eye piece in the door there is the calligraphed stencil of a rose. It makes me wince; I turn away. I check for other men. There's no one. If there was and they had known what they were looking at, they would laugh at me, so I knock. The door is immediately unbolted and steps apart to allow entry. The hall is sky blue and ironically cramped. To my left I see three more doorways, one is barred by a beaded curtain, touching the floor. Of the others, one is a closed door and one leads into a kitchen. I can see a dish-less sink. I imagine blood in it. I walk cautiously, taking off my coat and folding it over my arm. I sit down on an orange wooden chair; I cross my legs. It's familiar. I take in the kitchen, the bread on the counter, the pine cupboards, the flowered linoleum floor. People live here, I think. People are supposed to live here. I rub my thumb and fore finger together and smile a broad toothy smile, waiting. No one seems to like me, I think. Why would they make me work so hard, for so long, just to take everything away from me now? Why would they do to me what they have done to me today? I take a breath and knock gently on the door inside the door. It is also unbolted immediately and opened.

The room is as many rooms are. Not small. It contains a bed, wardrobe, drawers. No desk. The walls are white. The bed is blue, the sheets are blue. The covers are stripped back to open a line into the bed. The face before me is rounded, eyes are still small and soft, rounded, milky, and skin pock marked. A naked human being, but for black underwear and a stomach that does not hang, but swells like a small shell. Our manner is impartial, with recognition but not a firm memory of my name. She holds her back straight, even leans back. There are the usual markings on her skin in what looks like charcoal. It starts at the chest. It's a symbol like writing. A word, maybe, and a crown. We are expanding, which is normal, as we breath, before she begins to move. Yes, it is hot; she is laborious. I take a mouth breath. Hello, I think. She says nothing out loud. This is why she stays still and for her every time it is my turn for support. We're both not much for talking. I am mad, I think. I am going that way. She fiddles with her hair, lets one knee twist in to the other, each in the motion of waiting, out of habit, then remembers how I am and stops. The marks move on her stomach and sternum. She looks like she needs to go the toilet.

Hello, I say.

Any childishness dies away. I am lofty, I think. I don't need help for once. I can do this without anyone being here. They are the ones in control of both of us. I look around for cameras.

How are you? How have you been?

She stands in order to sit harder back on the bed. Her body crimps under the duress and the symbols with it. Over the elastic waistband of her pants, ribs rolling into the belly button, flat shut in the fold. She is flexible. I remember. It would be good to see her with some money. In hand. To buy cleaning products and alcohol and maybe a gun. I just assume they pay her. I held her ankles last time even though the position didn't make it feel very good and she obviously was uninterested by how slow I am. She sits for me. I am just trying to get my wits, so I can appreciate anything that I find myself doing. To put her at ease too. I must seem nervous, or peculiar. Another strange one. She must meet so many people who are not in the daytime, who are not nervous. If I could I wouldn't. I can remember notes. But there is no bartering. I would count money. Just three pieces of paper. I would tear the notes into thin strips, desperate to maintain the structural viability of each strip. I would then pop them in my mouth and let them hang over my lips like tails.

She reaches over the bed and from within the drawers pulls out a small plastic tube, it is grey. She squeezes a liquid from the tube and begins to rub it over her body. The writing dissolves into a smear that covers most of her chest. Her arms are skinny at the bicep, her shoulders are full and her arms not. Like all the blood in her is there. She finally gets up and gets me. She draws me close, onto the bed. I could do with a sleep, shake off the headache. In my hands the marks melt, with oil from the tube. But it is a dry melt and I hide my head in my shoulder. I nearly slip from the sheet. I see again the turquoise of the walls, the bedspread, the bed side cabinet. No strips of paper on my chin. My penis does not stir. I am like a cow in a field. Nothing continues on.

The air smells of talcum powder.

You smell like baby powder, she says.

It wasn't me, I mumble, with quieter sarcasm, so I cannot properly hear myself.

I feel the cushioned cover against my arse. I place a hand on her chest and try to retrace what was written. I keep myself down, flat on my back. I can feel each and every muscle in my body contract, as if a current passed through me and I were awaking fully from an abnormal nap. From my feet, to my thighs, stomach, shoulders and neck, my muscles are raised, inflamed, tight. I cannot ignore what is going on down below, and how central the attention is. I feel the stress rise, the excitement gone, the room a room. She places on it a prophylactic, a sour yellow colour. It slips over easily, and she pushes the remainder down. I look away from my body, to a spot on the wall. I peer down my nose, I look to the ceiling, the plaster is white. It has been un-evenly finished. Then a beeping, three beeps, in tone, and again. An alarm? Again, it bleets, in three tones. I can feel resentment well up inside of me. Where has my anger been? She stands up and grabs a small black box, from the same draw that held the tube, and holds it firmly in grip. It becomes pure liquid, black water and then disappears through her hand. My feet hav-ing touched the floor again my limbs start to lengthen and wrap around each other. Entwined, I don't know who is the bigger trick, the visitors or the staff.

She begins contact once more, with time to spare. Are the traditions of the Museum a punishment or a rite of passage? Or just the perks of the job? I turn on my hip, like some statue of an animal born incorrect, attached to itself, a white circular mess being sucked into a hole. Nothing continues to happen. I look at the bed beneath, her hand cupping me, propping me up in the air. I can see the top of an arse. I get no pleasure from the view. Across her lower back there is spread a tattoo. No, it is also a written mark. It is a foot wide at least. Black, washed green in the fade, perhaps sunlight had it once. A gem or an eye in waves of flames or vines spread out in all four directions, lick-ing out to her hips east and west and crowning short and sharp to the north and south. It is cheap and will last a lifetime. It's the same colour as the smear over her front. She places her hand on my back. Her skin is warm. It is not a touch of pleasure. I rub the line of her back, feel the ripples of her spine under my fingers, let my hand fall over the markings and cover the gem. She flinches forward, her nose touching my skin. I stop, do not move forward or back. I breath out, loudly, as if I have just left the city and arrived by the sea. Memories are as abstract as this room. Do you have any music or something? I say to myself, in my head. I wish I could scribble at this moment. This is when people get killed, I think, when they forget that it is not every day for everyone, and they forget they are with bad people. I hold my breath. The motion continues. My face contorts, I have become that child combatant once again, a darling soldier babe. I do not break silence; I clench my teeth. Nothing builds, nothing stirs. There is a knock on the door, a voice speaks through the wood. I can understand the message.

It is time up, it says.

That's completely fine, I reply, before she says anything.

I sink down onto the bed, unfurl, sit up and solemnly stand. First, socks on, one foot at a time. I take no notice.

I am sorry, the voice says from beyond the door.

I said its fine. Thanks anyway, I say.

I pull off the condom and place it on the dresser. My penis is greasy. I pull up my trousers, then step into someone else's shoes. I leave the room and do not look back at her getting ready once again. Outside the door, near the kitchen, a man is shepherded by, before I can see his face. He is older. I recognise his gait. Which team is he on? Who is leading him? It's too quick a shuffle for Kevin. Who else could it be? I know others. The man tries to look back toward me. I get a glimpse of his face; his eyes meet mine. This man is dying, he's been wounded somehow. He is going to speak to me. He is being moved.

Fellow... They're trying to keep us busy. They...

Then he's gone, behind the beaded curtains. I feel a solid shove on my back and I make my way out as fast as I can, quicker than how I had come. No one needs to push me. Slamming the door behind me, I think I really need to prioritise my health from here on in and make some changes to my lifestyle. I'm too stressed.

IX

The Guard on duty in gallery sixty-six is extremely impatient.

About time, he says.

For what? I reply. My shoes are rubbing.

Are you taking the piss? I know it was your go, but seven minutes late? You've eaten into time.

It doesn't really matter, does it? But I'm sorry, I say, with equal sincerity.

Well, it doesn't affect you, does it?

Sixty-seven minutes.

No, I suppose not, I reply.

Yea well, special day or not, I'll remember.

Do what you like, I reply.

I don't tell him I simply walked from gallery to gallery until I saw a face that was waiting for me and that's why I'm seven minutes late. I'm late because I'm not here. He's here and I've taken his place. He leaves and I am working in The Carcossa Gallery. It's a through-gallery, an en route, with one way in and one way out, doors opposing. It can be a slow post. The walls are lined with statuettes of various historical and mythical figures. Like every other bastard gallery. There are three pieces one would call statues here, given they are human-sized. There are three central plinth arrangements too, one of Dee's objects, one of pottery fragments, clocks and stones, and one of books. Three books. Books today. There is a bolted door in the wall. It is never been seen open, by me at least, and I watch for new things. No one can quite get their bearings as to where it leads, but it likely lines up with The Enlightenment Gallery, or, less likely, a passage into The Writing Room. So I will not be trying to open it this time. The door is bolted anyway, and it has visible shutters reinforced with iron bars. It's fair to say, this gallery is curated eclectically, and might be a dumping ground, a hodgepodge of trinkets. But these are galleries with a certain charm, those without a transcendent theme. If one is going by objects alone, it is not as obviously engaging as the more famous rooms, where visitors get the gist without even visiting and sometimes don't even go. But there is a mood to what is here, an accident of knowledge. Not a good mood necessarily, with each section telling distinct but interconnected stories. It is quieter place, electric lamp lit, rather than the neon strips. Without the threat of the inner elements, the objects, overwhelming the eye, it's easier to work.

I inspect the clocks. They do not tick. They are in a cupboard that is otherwise gutless. The books are better for just being three, laid on a table. The visitors can easily get bloated with the instinct to pretend to read everything. To lose time, as I do. Whole sections of our lives gone on the page. The books in this room are dubious. Dark arts and psyops. Though I won't veer into the occult as that's the theme of the gift shop. I'm still light-headed and content to rest. This is a fine room to do that. Whether the books here are authentic or not, they could be. You cannot retrace that anyway, and you cannot forge books without an original. These are originals, unburned, or they wouldn't be leafable. I survey the figurines. My crotch itches and my head aches. Not particularly unusual. What is unusual is that I know where these sensations began. I see visitors drying their eyes beside small statuettes. They have pride, blinking. The visitors are gulping, grinding teeth, seized by a feeling of remorse.

Statuettes of military heroes and heretics and such. Two large tears trickle down a face. These people are soft hearted as lambs. Soon they will be loosening or undoing their buttons, giving way. Only I was actually in the conflict, and they look down their noses at me. There are plenty of men and women, less orderly, who, I bet are still out there. And after drinking a bit, with the memories, go looking for trouble, and not work. I come straight home. I don't fool around and stray far from the galleries. I stay out of my head when needed. They don't even know how it is. I could kill them all and not remember any of it. I killed my own mother and father, figuratively. But I must moan. That is my job, and the weeping ones are never a bother.

The visitors in sixty-six tend to cluster around the first plinth, drawn to the objects associated with Joseph Dee, mathematician, astrologer and con artist, whom certain people seem to regard. There's controversy, I haven't followed it, but a lot of the copy on the labels is about conjuring up divine spirits using some of the displays, or some other drivel which misses the point. The labels talk about how the materials came to the Museum, through a chest they found buried. Then traced to the antiquary of Sir Bob Cotton, who was big before his country home was flattened. It's all made up. There's a large wax disc, called the 'seal of god', engraved with names and symbols, and it reminds me of the animal that bears its name. And there's a small projection you have to squint to see, where Dee, or the actor playing him, is using the seal for his 'shew-stones', where

he is allegedly seeing visions of divine beings unveiling the se-
crets of the universe. Fair enough. Useful information to have.

Perhaps I could do with shewing some stones of my own
today. There are two smaller discs also. The smallest, golden
disc is engraved with a so called 'vision of the four castles,' and
there's an obsidian mirror, originally from overseas. It's a cult
item for the visitors, who in their own way, conjure spirits. The
obsidian has a fitted case and a label in the hand of Horatio
Walope, who was a writer, and his note is translated on a card,
talking about human sacrifice. This phrase always makes me
think of how much can be considered a human sacrifice. To
the earth? To the appetites of permissiveness? To bad tempers?
There's a lot going on. There's also a small penknife, the end of
which is goldened. Dee pretended to make it so by dipping of
it into an elixir, proving alchemy. Another shitty trick. Today, as
ever, the gaggle of visitors gets bored and moves on through.

I stick my head out to see who is guarding the adjacents.
To the south of sixty-six is the small room of paintings. In it
I see Terry and I'm happy to recollect the team. Terry is Blue.
I'm in the right place. He is an old man, but daunting. More
than Kevin or any of the other old timers. He's a proper vet. He
has a plate in his head, they say. No one will ask him. There is
an element of volatility with Terry, but he seems to tolerate me.
Not that this ensures my safety. I get away without molestation
because of my service probably. He doesn't like Greg and did
try to bite him once. He will also often grab a handful of Greg's
arse and move him around with the grip. He doesn't trust him.
Terry is sat, looking into nothing. Surrounding his slightly bent,
strangely muscular frame are the small selection of canvasses
we were allowed to keep. They are connected to our collection.
They haven't been taken to another Museum. They say there are
other Museums just for paintings. I cannot imagine that's true.
It would be deathly boring to just look at bloody paintings all day.
I think it's just a good excuse to remove thousands of depictions
which might stir the visitors. They likely burn them. Our remaining paintings likely began as copies of lost masters. It's all a bit
symbolic for me, two dimensional things. Obviously made to
encourage the most passive doubt. To give the sense of letting
one's hair out, to relinquish tension in the eyes, but not the brain.
The paintings are of feasts and famines, cycles of the seasons,
farming folk with a touch of obesity nostalgia thrown in. Nothing of us, guarding. Nothing of squads ducked in formation,

sneaking through bushes. No implements of gaining information. No systematic eradication of enemies. Yes, there is some
tortuousness, but no depictions of how long you can go without
food. There are some outrages, and unnecessary cannibalism,
but no people snapping under the pressure. Nowhere in these
images is the very earth itself rejecting its animals. Just portraits
and pastoralism.

I look again, as Terry isn't looking at me, and think, there
are a few good ones though. Ira. Ira is the famous one, and it
hangs directly above Terry. I'd temporarily forgotten it. It is
quite dense. There's an armed figure in the centre, who the
label says signifies anger, personified, emerging with a sword
drawn, with an army swarming around her, from a tent and into
a landscape filled with violent scenes, including human figures
roasting over fires and naked figures being cut down with a
large knife.

At the feet of anger, her attendant is biting the leg of
a hapless naked victim and above her a gigantic hand holds a
knife. A great fire consumes a fantastical structure at right middle ground also, and a fearsome man is shat out by the fire, thick
all over. He has a heavy beard, that when you look closely, turns
out to be made of bees. His face looks then like a beehive, with
a lopped grin and chisel teeth at its middle. More dressed red
attendants flock to pin him down and are pushing syringes into
the back of his head, to restrain him and draw out a bit of ran-
dom brain, the label says. Up close the woman that is anger, in
the picture, seems to be having a stroke, or something, a mental
incident that has come from her character malfunctioning. She
looks like she's boiling, twitching. She looks like a baby grown
massive. No one in the picture is laughing. It's a quite interest-
ing painting, yes, as they go. Terry, rousing to see and recognise me, looks like he's of the picture and I am having another
moment of aesthetic inference. This is one I can enjoy, it's
bookless and not under the influence.

Alright, I shout at him.

Fink so, he grumbles, going still again.

I worked with Terry in the Mummies once and witnessed
why he has his reputation. He gave a small boy, he looked like
a waterboy, a nearly teen, a grim warning to stop touching a
sarcophagus. But the boy keeps touching, of course, and Terry
gives notice, and tells me to walk away. Alright I say. The boy
then actually leans down with his cheek and caresses the lid of

the stone coffin. Terry, like a massive purple fruit, grabs his wrist in his heavy, inescapable meat hook. The boy must've realised amongst that grip; he's made a mistake. With Terry's head shuddering, veins closing his scalp, he forces the boy's fingers in-between the crack of the lid and the box. The thing being solid rock weighs a tonne. Terry whispers to the child, right close to his face, that he is going to lift the lid and slam it shut, smashing all of his fingers to juice. The kid begins to wail and cry in pure terror of this mental gorilla majesty. Terry, in a surprising move, matches it, begins wailing too, straight into the child's face, in the middle of the Mummies, in front of thousands of hungry visitor mouths. Terry is above this boy like a broken machine, roaring, spit flecking into the little eyes and mouth. Of course, Terry's anger can lift the pure stone lid with one hand! The other still fixed on keeping the boy still. I don't know what happened, I walked off, as I was told to. It is simply inconceivable what ferocious ideas can ferment in the depths of a brain. I admire Terry. Even if you're not bitter by nature, it does make you mad when somebody puts on your own shoes to trample upon you. The visitors need guards like him. If anything, at least his is a vision of the future I can get with. His Ira.

I walk away, back to the Carcossa Gallery before I inspect the big three, the statues. They are not accidentally placed and have emblematic similarities to the paintings next door. Same author probably, but names of creators aren't displayed, obviously. Would be dangerous. The smallest of the three is Invidia, whom visitors tend to ignore. It's basically a woman holding a human heart, a real one, but plainly made up. She is having a vision, spasming, just like Ira. Blood is pouring from her nose. Then there's the middle statue, busier, Luxuria. It's basically a figurative nude female, again, exposed, hiding in the hollow of a tree. She seems unperturbed but is hiding, she's covered in something but is fine with it. Then Residia, surrounded so you can't get close. She lies asleep over the back of a donkey while a devil adjusts her pillow and around her other figures sleep at a table or in a bed drawn along by a strange duck-billed creature. They are an ambitious set. The maker must have been on one. Like me today. His mates probably mollied him. You can see slugs and snails, other animal representatives scattered through the statue bases. Residia has in her hand a small boy, nearly nude, his penis half-hacked off. Painfully thin, she looks sick. People can stare at her for hours. It's all a bit like a memory of things their parents have seen and through some genetic quasi-remembrance they somehow know.

I wander to the book table. One volume lies atop the other two, so you can't read them. Because you can't touch. The large, faded book above the others is shut and attracting no visitors. The cover is creamy, for it's a big, jaundiced thing. Normally this is the book at the bottom of the pile. I look around, there are no visitors near me or aware of anything but themselves. The label says, *Hastur*. It feels a bit rude reading someone's thoughts, but I open the book. As my fingers lift the pages, there is some movement in the gallery that I should take notice of, though I am sick of doing so, so I ignore it. I am on the precipice of reading something important. It's hard to even look up. The tiredness just gets in your bones. The day I've had.

The motion attempting to draw my attention is what seems to be a visitor walking through the gallery at a pace that makes no sense. It is too fast, too tall. I have no choice but to slam the book shut and glare.

Passing through my gallery, Greg does not stop to wave, or shake my hand, as is customary. Even if we have had a fallout, which we have not. In fact, he does not even acknowledge my existence. My feelings are hurt, even after all that has happened. I would think it incumbent upon him to apologise to me; for being different in the morning and for dosing me at lunchtime. But he worsens the discord by adding obliviousness to the afternoon. I'm going to kill that bastard, I think. He clears the gallery like a giraffe, taking large, familiar strides and then he is gone. I look again at the book and consider what is more intriguing, its contents or Greg. I think, well, it's about time I got him, given his determination. He needs a smack. Books can wait, Greg needs a dig. I dip into the next gallery and seek Terry.

Can you watch my post? I ask, without pre-amble.

Terry's neck cranes. He stares. He nods slowly.

How long? He asks, sluggishly. Why?

I think about lying to him, that I need the toilet, which I do.

I'm following Greg and when I catch him, I'm going to clump him.

About time, he replies and nods, smiling.

Use your little club, he adds.

x

If I'm caught off guard, that's fine. I have a few questions that need addressing. Following Greg, through Mesopotamia, I am almost left behind, until he knocks into a visitor, checking her and spinning her and continuing on. Unlikely to be an accident. He's no tourist, she can see. The visitor looks angrily after him, a small woman, with black hair that seems shifted as though it is a wig. She begins to bay and point her finger. A man joins her. He too begins to yap. Greg stops, his back to them. To listen? Another woman joins and the noise of humans complaining increases. Then another man. They are a cluster, a tourist party. They have a guide, who is dressed in a single block of colour, red, though his shirt is more faded than his trousers. He has the word *guide*, in a Germanic script, written on the back of his shirt. He speaks to them, listens, his face reddens to match his costume and he too begins to speak discordant babble in a language I do not recognise, that is not Germanic. Greg turns to face them. Slowly he regards them, one by one, ignoring me, again, utterly. He raises his right hand to his head, and taps his index finger against his temple. Then his upper lip starts to recede, exposing his upper teeth. Then his lower. He juts his head forward, his neck stretching, some hideous chimpanzee reversion. Then lips seal and he moves his hand towards his own neck. His middle and index finger fork and gently tap either side of his Adam's apple. Greg takes a sharp turn and leaves. The mob begins to look around them. For what? Knowledge of what has happened. Though they don't know and will not follow. It is a matter of moments before they see me, I think and I move on hurriedly, after Greg.

A sense of fun marks my pursuit, tracing Greg's curious abandon. Like the old days. Though back then I would actively try to catch. Notice nothing when there is nothing to notice, I say to myself, as I used to, out in the field. Fieldcraft was always something I enjoyed. Purposeful. I liked the open expanses. The after-surge landscape. Lovely how flat it could be, and yet, I could still hide. It wouldn't be folk like Greg I'd be stalking though. I was always squared away on prep. Prep prep prep. I would read maps, when one didn't have to draw them. I would scout. I had binoculars. I asked questions about what kind of people we were seeing. Most of the time, without much fanfare, I found them. Most of the time, when I found them, their imploring did not move me. Nothing moved me. And yet, I was not cruel. I've never been cruel. Work is work. A job is better done well if it's done at all. The Museum is different, hard to prepare. Greg is a clever walker. He always was, I'd guess. Tricky. The kind to be a principal when things were changing, and a nothing when they're not. Some people are like that. They can't wait for change. I was always much more for the times when things were the same. It's just timing. With time taken as awhile, being ingenious has limited use. The world has short shrift for clever people like Greg. Those who can't lift the pencil they write with unless they knock it off the table. Maybe he has understood that and changed. Rather than the other way round.

Greg is climbing stairs, out of Mesopotamia. They are crowded and I can only see him because he is so much taller than the bulk of visitors. This is the afternoon push, when the crowds really swell, coming out from the cafes and restaurants stuffed and food drunk, joined by the lazy, those waking up late on holidays, finally breaching the Museum gate. Together, they are indiscernible. They become the public. It takes presence of mind to avoid. On the stairs, surging down, the visitors are pressing into the few cases on the walls or landings. Here a child bashing a rattle against plastic glass, there an elderly woman eating mouth-open before a precious gold tree frog. There a man's belly bursting from a shirt, rubbing others, being scratched, being used to prop a monopod. The oddest phenomenon of the rush, that human features homogenate. They aren't together for warmth, as they used to be, when they couldn't defend themselves. Not for the objects either, but for the abstract desire to be together. And not in a good way. To be a mass. As if they like to be packed physically as they are in their minds, drawn to the Museum because of its narrow corridors, small doorways. And we reciprocate, as though the Museum was designed for this purpose, its internal architecture being its reason, not the things contained throughout.

Greg has escaped the staircase, I glimpse, three floors up, off a landing, taking us into the Mummies. He is seeking the worst mobs. These galleries are where the throngs are harshest and most dazed and baffled. There are no frescos, no crosses, no models of hares and doves, no paintings. Nothing delicate. Just human remains. The visitors are desperate to see the bodies, the dead husks of other people. I reach the gallery and push my way in. In the Mummies they are all leaning over. Greg is skipping through them like sport. The Mummies are trouble because they make the visitors agitated. Because they seem real? It's hard to believe these skeletons were once encased in flesh. Where did it all go?

I briefly lose Greg but catch him again, in the midst of a conversation, with a visitor. I'm surprised he's stopped. It delights me to see the visitor is a member. It is obvious he is a member. An absolutely type, an awful, wealthy person. They pay a little for privileges. A member to the eye, down to his attire. Appropriate he is in this gallery, stopping Greg like he is a host, and not a guard, and a normal guard like me or Kevin, and not a mad guard, like Terry. He is not apologising for his interruption; he is demanding something. Greg holds up his hand, silence, and oddly it seems as though he is speaking to the man as though he knows him. That is until Greg reaches down in one swift gripping and yanks up his shirt. It exposes his entire upper body, from his belly to his neck. The cloth sits over his head, like some ancient, funereal mask. He doesn't move, frozen. Nor does Greg. Nor does another visitor stop, or scream, but they look. We can all see his white belly, the upper crop of black hair, his breasts, the rawness on the skin from blistering tanning treatments, his crab ladder. The stillness after such an outrageous act has a purpose. I have never seen a guard do anything as provocative as this. It's not a fight or a threat, not a slap or a wrestle. It's a quiet disgrace. The visitors are all staring at Greg and this sculpture of a man, pacified. A heightened dead moment, in this small country building of other people. Greg has made a fleshy mummy. Greg hesitates, and I think he's going to stab him, slit open his fat belly. Greg walks away. The visitors crowd, as the man begins to peel his own clothing from his face, they begin to touch his exposed stomach with their fingertips, as though they were examining the texture. I do not stay to see what happens. I do not want to find out why the man did not defend himself.

At the far end of the Mummies is a small wooden door leading to what I think is a staff toilet, hidden in what looks like a cleaner's cupboard. I see Greg go into this door and wonder; has he just been running to go to the bathroom? You need a key to enter, and inside is just two cubicles. In each cubicle, I recall, is a board with a hole below. I saw no key in Greg's hand. I never use this hole because it's a cesspit and I saw once a swarm of something, small, moving, in the dark. I've heard in the public toilets, the ones the visitors use, there are instructions that the seats should always be sprayed with a strong insecticide. I'd think the insecticide is to act as an aerosol. The stench of these visitor toilets is outrageous. I reach and open the door, it is unlocked. It opens into space. It's no toilet. I feel the visitors push behind me, they will be looking in, they have appetites to serve. Not a toilet but another stairwell, empty. It is a staff escape. There are these all over, but I've never needed to use one. It's just concrete steps and iron railings. Greg seems to have gone. It is either up or down. I listen but do not hear steps. Before I can close the door, I feel a swift and solid impact on the side of my head. As I slump, I pull shut the door behind me.

I stand still and wait. I can hear the visitors swarming outside the door, but it is quiet inside. No sign of Greg. I feel groggy, in a different way than before. I close my eyes. I am now alone and must make a decision. Go back outside and find out whom, or what, has struck me, and ruin them. Or, because I have followed Greg, because I believe I have caught him out somehow, stay put, heading up, or down. I wonder, has Greg led me on because he has seen me as his admirer? He wants to teach me something? Or he wants to share with me something he knows? Perhaps he has started something appalling, and that is why the public have hit me, if they have, and if I go outside, who knows? I might be in trouble. Yet, what will be above me now, or below me? I think it wise I stop still in this empty staircase, and not follow on. Be still. A rest is best, because I am preparing for what might be next. I know Greg knows I might do this. I know he knows I know he knows. My eyes are closing already, so I sit. I reach down to cushion with my hand and then touch the base of my head. My fingers come away wet. Greg, I think. There are some mysterious persons—always the same ones—who stand like sentinels at every crossroads in your life. What a captivating day in the Museum. I slump against the door. I wouldn't say I am knocked out, knowing what I know about the human head, but I do close my eyes and accept a small force of obscurity which wants to take me. I meet, head on, the drowsiness so convincing that I could call it a prompted sleep. I hear a sharp crack, a bang, from the Mummy Gallery, through the oak door, but I feel very safe. My mouth opens and I close my eyes.

Is there a chance to be finally recognised in the dark? But the room was always supposed to be dark. That is the purpose of the room. There are others where it is so light you cannot see. People often perish in the wild because of unexpected drops. The ground gives way. It need not be a cliff face. It can simply be a slope. I've seen it, even though it was dark. I can't imagine I will go, but I've seen it happen to others. A great number of others. All of them, within reason. The cloud was so large it was excessive. It was like the ground had made a new ground, a mirror of itself, above. And it made a night like this. Darkness as if the light has gone out in a room that is locked and sealed. A deep ocean darkness above the water.

A hand lain across my brow, I don't start, just slowly open my eyes to a lesser dim. Between the warm, dry fingers I can first make out a single orange cat's eye above me. It's a nightlight, an emergency light. Because of the unnamed danger, I feel sickly. The mitochondria before my eyes look like pests surrounding a ceiling, about to dart into its centre, above me. I have been moved. I am not in a stairwell. I have a touch of the dream I'm leaving behind. No one wants to read about dreams, but it's not a dream so much as another remembrance. There's was a valley. I am above it. One would assume on a hill. The cloud has settled, but was fresh. Ash on the grass. It's dusk, I am wondering why anyone would build their home in a dip in the earth. We've come to collect something. There are tiny orange lights that must be the windows piercing the gloomy, irregular houses below. I hear something load. Then the hand on my face begins to moisture and I am too aware of it to be concerned with the vision. I am happy to be cut off, but now must deal with the awkwardness of the hand. It is not trying to restrain me. It is not trying to comfort me. It is simply touching, something like an extended attempt to keep one's balance. I must take a decision to move the hand. But. On the hill I show myself attentive, considerate, tactful. As one is at eighteen, and an orphan, of sorts. When we bring them out, they aren't surprised. They had been expecting it. They had decided to stay in their homes knowing this would be the way. I wonder then, lining them, why the sons and daughters of polite society seemed to always wear mild cases of acne and a few too many pounds upon their frames. They weren't even fat in the formal sense, just soft limbed. The younger ones especially. The cause was surely their diet. One girl, her big red and green pyjama stripes lay across her like a robe. She carried her weight superbly. I'd got used to skinniness. Even in such a short time. The compassion in her astonished me. It was like she had been born late. I reach up and peel the fingers from my face.

That'll do. They move as though they had never been there, without the faintest hint of a muscle contraction. The man above me, and it is immediately clear it is a man, is foregrounded by the light above him. I cannot describe the shape of him. There is something reassuring though. He wears a mask, but of cloth. Perhaps a black scarf, wrapped to cover the chin, jaw, mouth, teeth, tongue and nose. His eyes are free, looking down on me. There is something sacrificial in his bearing, some sense of benevolent regret.

He slowly places one single finger, I would guess the middle, on my chest. He then bows it upwards, as though it were a drill about to bore down through the sternum, missing my heart. The room seems to get dimmer, which is strange, as my eyes are adjusting. I beckon him in. He might think I were allowing him to kiss me. Carefully he leans over, bending at the hips. I realise how tall he is, and thin. When his ear is next to my mouth, I whisper. He raises up just slightly, so we are side by side and eye to eye diagonally. He seems to be thinking me over. Impatience is already creeping in.

I don't care why you're here, I say.

His hand curls into an overtly cautious, careful thumbs up. Then he leans down to speak to me.

I think we were meant to meet, he says, muffled. He's smiling.

I don't think so, I snap back, a touch too loud.

He slowly shakes his head. I shrug. His eyes glint. They could practically spill themselves, his eyes, aqueous humour leaking, naturally, like a pimple squeezing itself, through the jelly lid. I don't doubt he has the power to regulate his eyes at will, the way I might've once adjusted night vision goggles. I can see this single thing about him, which confirms him as Greg, that when he wants to withdraw himself from others, to move into himself, he starts with his looks. I know this because I myself have attempted to practise such a method. I had learnt it from an army doctor I knew.

Greg.

Yes, Greg replies.

What are you up to? I ask.

Nothing much, he replies.

That's good, I say, seriously.

Will you come with me please? he asks.

Yes, I reply. I've been trying.

I know. Thank you.

Where are we? I ask.

Your cupboard, he says.

We are in The Enlightenment Gallery, then. Not the gallery itself, but the cupboard adjacent to room two. The last time I was in here was with Rebecca. Everyone laughs at me behind my back, I am sure. But she led me here, having heard about me and the cupboard. Then I'd shut the door behind us. What is the significance of your neck, I would ask her, noticing her small scar. It's all in your head, she would say. Then she would show me her teeth. I liked that. Her sharp teeth. In a certain way her movements were passionate. Her contempt for me. Her opinion, dispassionate but firm, matched my own.

Follow, says Greg.

He helps me up and leads me through a small door, hidden in the wall of the cupboard. I can feel no handle ahead, but I see we are at the bottom of a staircase and it is the same staircase as before. He's dragged me down the stairs? We are not going back up, and out, not into The Enlightenment Gallery either, through the people, and not back to the Mummies. There is a long tunnel onward, a passage with a low ceiling. I feel surprisingly able, crouching, and shadow Greg, as instructed.

What is happening? I ask.

Follow, he replies and leads on so quickly that I have no choice.

I glance back at my cupboard. There is a pressure in such a small space. You get so used to the crowds you become happy pressed up against somehow who thinks poorly of you. Rebecca is so clever and beautiful. It's ridiculous how much people better people are in the pitch darkness with their hands wrapped around you. It's like childhood longing come to pass just after you've forgotten what you always wanted. To bond with someone more influential than you, who you could just snuff out, like pulling the cord in an accessible toilet, or leaving a bag unattended. It's almost irresistible.

The last time I was here... I mumble.

I know, I know, I hear him say, into the murk ahead. Rebecca told me.

A corridor I have never seen before. I thought the cupboard just ended with the cupboard. Greg seems to have lit the
way ahead of us with a phone or small torch. Up here, I am
with him, back there, with Rebecca. What is better? Two
crowded bodies. The closest we got to visiting. I wonder why
she did? I knew it was probably the awkward secret which had
attracted her to me in the first place. She was bored also. But if
I saw her out on the galleries, she would barely flinch. A smell
filling the whole closet in one moment and then I was used to
it, as it mingled with an equally pleasant, vague scent of mould.
She knew what I did before, it was Greg who told me that. And
she is like Greg, I realise now. A pure-bred functionary. No
choice but to flip or be one of those daughters of society I had
pulled from their homes. She reviled me because of that.
Perhaps now she'll be able to get her hypothetical revenge.

Follow, Greg repeats.

My legs ache, as I stoop. Then the light of Greg's phone
disappears. Another door opens before me and Greg's long
fingers can be seen holding it in place.

This way, he says.

I step out and am in the Post Office passage. It is empty.
We walk by the doors. Greg is aware but seems unworried
by how perverse our presence is here. I have a sense it'll be fine,
as Terry is covering my post, and he is an old timer, but then I
realise how absurd this is given what has happened. Perhaps the
Museum is in lockdown. Perhaps it has been cleared. Perhaps
they have armed Terry and Kevin and Rebecca. And found Mark.
Perhaps the visitors have done what I have long suspected they
might and overcome the guards. I am off post all the same, as
though Greg were the curator, giving me orders. I pass where
I entered this morning, and hesitate, Greg keeps on. At the last
door of the hall, he stops and opens it. Nothing is locked to us.

The room is empty. The walls are black, the ceiling too. There is but one thing in the room. A window, facing down, in the floor. It does not look Museum made. The edges are roughly cut and the glass itself is fogged and chipped. Greg places his finger to his lips.

It took us four years to make this, he whispers.

I can see hatred on his face. His lips nearly curl back again.

They never noticed.

Then pride as he swallows.

They became satisfied, he sighs.

Greg lies down and I lie with him, before he tells me to. He looks down, through the glass, and I look with him, eventually, opening my eyes.

XII

We are staring through glass that is one way. We are watching a scene from above. What are we looking at Greg? I ask. I don't expect him to answer. I also don't expect him to undo his belt. He's relaxing himself.

I look down upon a man. He is one of four bodies. It is all horrendous. I can see him trying to lie still, as though the pain will leave him should he manage to be completely still. For a second, he seems to find this relief, his face masked in a pulsing breath, momentarily overcoming the unrelenting suffering that has been inflicted upon him. But then he moves again. Not just because the shock will not keep the motionlessness he wants, but, it seems, because the trembling aftermath of what he has suffered comes to him as a thought. I can see something flashes over his face as he remembers. I look around, above him. Nothing but a plain wooden ceiling. Panelled over concrete. He is remembering implements perhaps, or a narrative of the work they have done to him. The shape, length and colour of the instruments, where on his leg they have begun, where they have pierced the skin and the direction they have begun to sew. So his body moves, involuntarily or otherwise, and in so doing the scabs on his arms, which I assume must also cover his back, become irritated, breaking into little wet red patches that makes them appear from a distance like bacteria multiplying under a microscope. I see some of the fluids are more yellowish, or made so against his skin, perhaps translucent. Not burns though, each wound is intended in its shape, small crosses or straight lines. Markings. I can see the burns on his hands, around his knuckles and fingers, still dusted with ash. These types of wound are different.

There are four beds in the otherwise empty chamber. Each bed is occupied. Each occupier is covered in an almost translucent gown that lies on them like a sheet. The colouring of the sheet, from left to right, descends from bright and clean to almost entirely pink. Each occupant is bound with strong straps fashioned around their hands, feet and neck. While the body on the left can strain against those binds, and does, the one on the furthest right seems stuck to them, healed into the leather. It is the centre right body that I have first become fixed on. I was sure the body furthest to my right was still. Like meat, rather than a human still alive. This body, in fact, is perhaps without its skin. They are therefore in a kind of ascending order of damage. One to four, left to right.

They lie without sound. The silence resembles respite, as though the four occupants are grateful. But we can hear them not making noise. We can hear what is happening below, it has been microphoned, audible in the room, though the auditory links are not visible. Maybe just not being wounded at this moment is good. I look for the source of light in the room but cannot see one. The light is strangely even throughout the room, not the corners, nor the beds, nor the roof is lit any more or less than the other. The colours, besides the colours of flesh, are indiscernible, blue perhaps, or a dirt green. Or grey. I can make out the smallest movement on the body to the furthest right, the movement of eyes in their sockets. But even more pronounced is the rapid, darting motion because it is framed so tightly, as the sockets have clearly suffered massive damage and have puffed up into black, grazed bruises. I feel ill. It's clear that the wounds to this bodies' eyes itch. Each glance, it seems, to the others, to the walls, brings forth a further twinge of pain that lasts because it cannot be expressed, or at all escaped.

The first two occupants on the left have their eyes tightly shut, as if they had had them previously pried open, and literally so, both having purple lesions on their foreheads and upper cheeks, though without swelling or indents. They close them tightly, like they might go blind otherwise. It occurs to me then that the third and fourth occupants may have indeed been blinded, and that the rapid, desperate glances of those in the latter beds are the looks of sight lost, of looking for something in the dark. The third body seems braced against something, squinting, as though it has seen flashes coming, or a vehicle driving for it.

These are small, nurtured movements, attempted while trying not to break the cuts that lace its exposed legs and arms and face. Sudden explosions of light are hitting their eyes. Taking in these finer details, I see how they have been brought into states of despair, in order, in careful hierarchy, measuring severity. Is this punishment for crime, scaled? Or is this about the passage of time? Is each forced to see what is to befall them? Would each know their determined future? Or are they able to change their order? If not, then is the fourth bed accompanied by the great relief of knowing you are soon to drop off the conveyor? Unless another gallery lies ahead of this one?

What have they done? I ask Greg, quietly.

A convulsion happens from the first body, furthest left. Despite the relative lack of blood outside the skin, this body accommodates new pain. The wounds are designed to not draw blood. I see its right shin, blackened, florid. It has been cracked and softened, but not broken or bludgeoned. The body is trying to cope, and the body to its right, the second down, has a similar leg wound, but the bone is clearly broken, piercing the skin. It seems designed so that the onlooker, those to the left, can assess the damage from the corner of their eye. Or maybe in the first moments of being tied down, or the last of being dragged out. Maybe these bodies arrive unconscious. The only other outward damage on the body to the far left is that the fingernails are missing.

I spot a blemish on the floor of the room. It is teeth, I think. The body in the middle left has spat them, or they have been dropped from an implement that pulled them. That jaw is misaligned too, visibly unset. Whereas the last body is one whole wound, a mass of sores, metal inserts and numbness, the first two are pinpointed, even healed in places. Wounds on the second body seem surrounded by white scarring, fat and puffy. They have healed and been reopened. I imagine them all stood, without these sheets, and how they must have appeared to themselves, in a mirror. It appears they are looking up towards us. I listen for any noise, any groan or vibration. Anything signalling a call. Then I realise beneath the window, almost underneath us, there must be a door. How else would anyone access this gallery? I note a change in colour on the floor. There is an amorphous, borderless shape, directly beneath Greg and I. It looks as though this part of the room has been washed, inflected, with a luminous, perhaps toxic material. Or the room is just barely aslant, and everything that has happened at the beds or above has run off down to pool and dry.

A sudden movement, perhaps only a foot, or even a toe, from one of the beds, alerts me to change. The vision has enthralled us. How long have we been watching them? Mere seconds possibly. Greg is still, he has not looked at me. Not once, and not one word. His face seems impassive. A smell reaches us, or is new, penetrating the glass. To see it, is to see it. To smell it is to realise it is true. The bodies below have evacuated their bladders and bowels at something. Nothing drips, no further colour is visible. All that is noticeable is that the third body's hands, blackened from burns, without fingernails and with deep cuts up into the skin, between each finger, seems to reach to cover its groin.

I hear the steps sometime after the smell. The grating noise of a key in a lock below us, where there is a door, it turns out, seems impossibly loud. I naturally fear us getting seen and caught and joining in. The lips of the bodies start to move, in different stages of cracked and bleeding disorder, so that blood begins to spill, slightly and bright, painting their lips like lipstick. Into the room steps a small, hunched figure wearing a dark green pinafore and carrying a bucket and a white plastic case. It is wearing a white wig, or has curled white hair, tight to its head. It cannot be more than five feet tall. Its uniform rests over its whole body and we cannot see its feet. There is a noticeable sagging of the bodies, though small, they are obviously relieved.

The figure seems obscene because it seems able to move. Yet it does not move much, and maybe isn't supposed to. Its head blends into its upper body, if its torso can be understood from its trunk. It tapers from its hair down to the floor, and it's looking for something. Then it places down the case and pulls from within a spray bottle. It squirts some sort of liquid on a tiny part of the floor and then crouching over, with a troubling swiftness, wipes. It then, never once looking at the bodies, as though it were fixed or trained to look upon the far wall, or into space, begins to spray the feet and legs of the body in the first bed. What seems like cleaning fluid is jetted onto the feet of the body, and then wiped off. The wiping moves up the leg, and onto the blackened shin and the body opens its mouth.

The cleaner works its way across all four of the occupants. At times the spray bottle is refilled, and then shoots out in its tiny action. Sometimes the scabs come clean off under the wiping, leaving behind cuts or pink patches of skin. Other times they bleed. Sometimes it has to rewipe pus, and will do so until it ceases weeping. At times, as if accidentally, the cleaner will push and pull the bodies, each terrible minor shift causing immeasurable pain. Each time, their mouths open silently. The implement, which I assume, but cannot see, is a rag, catches fingers, toes, lumps, welts and raised cuts. And then the bodies in one sudden heave, are lifted, and their backs scrubbed, their arses wiped. Once that liquid mess has been drained and dried, then the body is allowed to lie flat and with imperceptible quickness a new sheet is thrown out over them while the old is pulled in. As though what was underneath can't be exposed to open air. Or to someone watching on. Aside from us. How strong this small figure is. They seem limitless. For a moment, in lifting the fourth body, I see the cleaner's face. I recognise them.

I've seen them before, I whisper to Greg.

His eyes grow wide and he places his finger to his lips, staring at me with an arch seriousness. The cleaner, whom I recognise from outside the Relief Gallery, does not appear to hear me. I try to remember them. Just a forgettable face. I do not remember such a malign shape. When the four bodies are cleaned, their lungs visibly heaving under their sheets, sweat mingling with cuts already running, the cleaner walks backwards to the blind spot and removes a clipboard and sheet. A pen clicks, and the sound of the nib on the paper, imprinting into the board appears audible but I'm likely imagining. The bodies are becoming stiller. In wiping the face of the third body, the cleaner has offset its nose, which must have been previously righted after breaking and is now veering to the left, with mushy cartilage. I am unsurprised to see the body doesn't seem to notice the change. On the first body, the lungs are not settling, not returning to their shallow breaths as quickly as the others. Some wetness around the eyes, open, but not too swollen. The body is hyperventilating. The cleaner ceases her notes and as an afterthought walks back over to the body, having removed something from the case. She lays a cloth over the eyes and mouth of the body. The cloth is white, not dirty, the brightest thing in the room. It is laid gently, covering the whole face like a mask. I then suddenly wonder what does the face look like, as I could see it moments ago but have now forgotten. What is the face beneath the cloth? What age, and gender? And yet I cannot take my eyes from this blankness. A block of white cloth.

With their other hand, the cleaner begins to gently pour a clear liquid from an unmarked receptacle upon the cloth. It would be water, but it falls too slowly from the jug. The body strains, but not so much. There is no sound of gurgling, just a faint struggling at the bonds. Its heavy, laboured breathing has been quelled. Now it is clearly battling to breath at all. I want to look away and I feel out for Greg at my side. He is gone. I turn carefully and can see him at the doorway, quietly turning the handle, his face impassive.

That's enough, he sighs.

XIII

Powered by some terrible suffering and not a machine or a virtual inanimation, the purple sun goes down over the staff garden. To be outside is unnatural.

I endure pains in my legs from the squatting and lying, and my head aches still, and I want to swing my arms about to shake something loose, but instead I just sit next to Greg. I don't want to knock a plant out of its pot. Greg sits, almost indifferent, on a bench, next to the waterhole, the fish pond, and for a time, says nothing. We are alone, of course. Moments ago, we were not. Outdoors, with the dander of the trees slowly raining down, and the sound of the visitors queueing and griping just a wall beyond, the recent past feels imaginary.

Just a cleaning today, Greg begins.

I saw, I say, defensively.

Greg seems to have put on weight. He fully embodies the air of a man who has done me a favour.

There will not be another other day, he replies.

I shake my head. This goes without saying and yet he's saying it to me. The purpose must be to convince me of something. It is always the way with professional revolutionaries.

It didn't seem familiar to you? he continues, tenderly.

No, I reply. I have never been there before.

Greg nods. I tell him the truth, as much as that is possible. I can sense what is coming.

We can't always be on the galleries, he says.

He tells me something I know to obscure that which he thinks I don't. He more of the Museum than I can ever could imagine. And his newfound wistfulness is getting on my nerves.

Yes. I know, I say. Same old same old.

It's not that, he interrupts. Not just that.

He sits forward. If Greg is nervous, it's not about me. That much is now clear. What am I to him, now? When he can see the permanence of his fresh start before him like a new country, with its flag and land and populace and style, and history? A history of a new planet even. With the objects to prove it. Who am I to put people in their place? And what I do appreciate, seeing the bodies on the beds, those four people, those interchangeable individuals, allowing Greg to feed me clues, is that my suspicions about repetition have long been reasonable. I am not the main guard in these barracks. This is not about the people I reduced and eradicated in the cloud those years back. Nor does it matter that were Greg and I to lower ourselves to a fistfight he would die with his skull smashed into pieces on the floor. This is simply the first time I am grateful for the fact that this isn't about me.

If we are on the galleries we are rebuilding. Do you follow? He asks.

Yes. I can see how you think you were. But not me.
I was just working.

That's not true, Greg says, and there's the fervour, getting ahead of himself.

You know things I do not, I say, interrupting.

You think that just because we get used to it. Because, if that's all you felt, it would all lose its effect. People can get used to anything, he says, and goes too far, even for me.

Do you know them in there? I ask, interrupting him again.

Greg shakes his head. He is being frank and pathetic again, finally, and yet I can't think of a follow up question about those on the beds.

It doesn't matter whether I know them, he says. We've decided. We are just not doing this again. Even if it makes, to them, an impression. Even with its internal logic, and its tradition. And I know you understand the principle. We don't need it anymore. This is the last day of it.

I nod.

We're going to level it, he says.

The intensity of the flowers in the garden makes me feel queasy. My body has had a full day. I've never liked strong aromas. Visitor smells, perfume, other people's odours. It's a small place, the garden. We are sitting next to a great spider-domed banana tree and it is obviously designed to mimic the Grand Hall as a canopy. It feels offensive, to pretend its natural.

They're real you know, Greg says.

I know that, I answer. Those poor objects, I say.

The plants, he replies, and I laugh out loud.

His bearing, once so intractable, even feeble, now attempts to be stern and aristocratic, and returns again to a new kind of frailty. This is the only kind of change in people. Ideas that produce circular appearances. Greg is getting ready to work. To save us from our routines, whether we like it or not. I see before me a brutish face that has nearly spared me rhetoric. He knows I've been at the front end I suppose.

You've noticed the morning dust before, he says.

Everyday. As we eat.

He raises his eyebrows and we watch the particles of dander floating in the air around us. It looks like insects, but there are no flies in the garden. Too many spiders to eat them. No insects at all that I can see.

And the visitors? I ask, knowing the answer.

There are no visitors, he says, unamused.

Staff?

We are all staff, he replies, and again I smile.

Why are they doing it so slow?

You tell me? says Greg, full of love.

Greg seems to sense relaxation as I feel déjà vu. This is a metaphor for the differences in our characters. How lucky we are to be outside. I think about making a move for him.

We are bringing it down today, he says, loud enough for anyone to hear.

It feels as though he is going to make a literal gesture, like a salute. It is like he is chewing something imaginary. Either he wants to explain to me the day has been a test, and that is why it needed to be so circuitous, or he wants to ask me to help in a more active way. Has it all been a warning, or a request? He knows I am not against change for the sake of change.

Some people just suffer in silence, I say, to mimic his manner.

I can imagine, replies Greg.

It's fine, I say. Better it comes down so you can put it back up again.

My attempt at humour, to let him get on. You have to give people a way out I've found.

Yes, he replies. They used to wall the workers up when they finished with them.

Wall them? I ask.

Lay them into the foundations. Between the bricks. Cement them in.

I know he wants to tell me to come along, even if I stay impartial. I might be useful. Then I might stay with some relative of his, on the right side of things, afterwards, well away from the Museum. It is quiet down there, out there, he'd say, quite peaceful, safer. Aside from the occasional raid by one of the gangs, I'd reply. If we both go, it'll be better for them, he might say. More mouths to feed. I'd nod and touch his arm in thanks but forget the invitation. There will be gangs in the woods. Gangs in the fields. Gangs in the basement.

I look at him and he has already picked on my lack of words. He is getting ready to get up and head back for the shove.

Yes, it's all right. Just go back to your gallery, he says, disappointed.

Enthusiasm is impatience, I reply, and now he smiles.

Greg and I, the banana tree shielding us, the last two staff members to visit the garden. This is unusual, to know when a last moment of anything has come. It'll take them years to build again, and I'll be old by then.

We will not harm each other, and this is enough so that we might help each other. He departs before me, busying himself to seem important as he leaves. I must decide. Leave, pushing past the guards at the gates without stopping for my effects. Or re-enter for the last time.

For curiosities sake.

XIV

I hear the cries crossing the courtyard. I enter through the front entrance. The doors have been broken. It's inviting. The queue is gone. The Great Hall, if anything, seems busier than before, but with burning and ruin. A visitor runs past me with a significant headwound. They don't make it to the doorless exit. But it's another visitor who stops them. It's like certain veiled spots in a dream have come to life. It's a painting, and the light is right, finally. There are screams but they mingle, so I can't say I'm disturbed about the suffering of any specific individual. There's too many of them. I wouldn't guess how many. A population. I feel I have in fact dreamed, or seen, this before, and not a version of such a scene out in the hills. But no one wants to hear about my dreams. I've seen uprisings before, sure. But in a Mueum? It's to be expected that during a full life one might witness a few. It is like the old days, a bit. Things are flying through the air; objects have been smashed, dragged from galleries by people who shouldn't have the strength. It's all a motion. They are all swimming in it. What I have never seen is so many people turmoiling together in such a slight space. We are indoors, after all. A constituent element of the Museum. To be roofed and protected from the elements. But they have made the Great Hall feel small. This is what it must've been like in a shopping centre during the surges. Yet I do not feel in personal danger. If anything, I feel ignored. This is the most underestimated consequence of having principles.

I walk the wall nearest to the entrance and half-hide to watch the miraculous unfold all around me. The mob has its own energy. How novel. This is history happening to itself. I am witnessing a catastrophe, again, and I feel no longing for everything to stop. What has escaped cannot be stuffed back in. This is already normal. But that is typical of the Museum, to absorb even that which destroys it as a display, or exhibition of events, neatly tailored for understanding. I have been preparing for knowledge for such a long time. Seven troubled years, finally, have a justification. At my feet, I see frantic movement, and the most extraordinary sight. A small creature lifting a lid. It's a tunnel door, or a ventilation duct, and the thing is crawling itself in, raising the fused metal circle as though it were paper, and slipping beneath to disappear. A child, covered in blood, escaping the upheaval, or a little demon, all wet and happy. This is also familiar. Either I did this myself once, or I saw it in one of the paintings upstairs.

They all look small, the visitors. At times they swell togeth-er, at others it is obvious they are inept at harming each other. This makes it all slower, watching for things, grabbing and tearing and biting. Sometimes I see them fall and crush each other, against the floors and walls. They are ripping through the galleries like a flood or fire. But no such thing has happened, it's all relatively organised. I can just about discriminate visitor throngs from guards, who are reacting and surviving. I can see other visitors trying to escape and panicking, and guards happy at the opportunity to remove anyone, and hosts trying to help and dying. The fakes and doubles are in various factions, mixing with those who are not, and those in between. The leaders of the chaos, who have possibly planned it, are perhaps losing their stomachs. Depends on their stomachs I suppose. You can get used to anything. And I bet there's still visitors at the front gate trying to get in. It's not a controllable crowd.

No one is interested in the contents of the Museum any longer. There is very little time to look upon the objects with wonder and reverence. Such information seems a bit precarious surrounded by screaming. I see a statue brought down, it's the Roman emperor Elagabalus. Was this an accident? He has fallen and smashed and has definitely crushed a few legs on impact. I've logged over hundreds of hours waiting for that to happen, for someone to bump into a statue of an emperor, and to witness the full viciousness of the visitors to be allowed out. I'm jeal-ous. It is all a natural illumination, coming in through the glass ceiling, massive and dimming with the purple sun above us. It is, in a way, joyful and persuasive. Because it's finally authentic. Something true has come to life. Good on them.

It does not shock me to see a small horde trampling others underfoot, or many grabbing one, to beat them and pull their clothes from their bodies. There's so much to see. The crowd that once were visitors don't seem to mind me, but then I find I've torn and taken off some of my uniform. The visitors are being stabbed but they are getting hold of everyone, weaponed or otherwise, and ripping them apart. Some have been fore-warned, it seems, as I was. Why or where it has come from seems unimportant. I don't keep up with the news. No one can say they weren't warned, walking around the Museum, civilisation to civilisation, room to room. For what have they, and we, been looking at but war, insurrection, destruction, skinning, beheading, torture. Fresh starts. And it's understandable that this begins again with a brutal naivety, but I must admit, once underway, it has its charms. It's easy to get swept up as a spectator. It's not as though we can't understand where each of us has got our ideas from.

In the middle of the hall, at the foot of the stairs, there comes an artificial glow that cuts through the crowd. It is a high-powered torch. It is a curator, the fellow I met earlier, and a small group of guards surrounding him. He has before him, a little display. How brilliant. It is a stone. A thin stone plate, in his palm. It is a plinth, a kind of maquette. In the centre of the slab is something else. I walk over, touching people out of my way for the first time, and that feels quite good, taking my back from the wall, remembering talents. It is a sliver of something like a human tendon. The curator has this in his hands. A disappointment, I thought it'd be a magic relic or a holy book. I see the curator's face; one side is awash with blood. It pours from a large wound, which seems yet to be coagulating. You think he'd find a cupboard and wait it out. This is not his forte. I look back at the plate. It is a human cheek on a piece of metal. Now I understand. The curator is carrying his own face before him like an offering. The guards around him, they are fighting people away, and they are shouting. They yell again and again.

The Museum is closed, make ways to the exit.

Again, fantastic stuff. What an institution. His cheek reminds me of a child's cheek, like a bit of ordinary animal skin. I watch the curator call for his megaphone and think, in wonder, how intellectuals can do it. He draws himself up to address the crowd. I can see the pain on his face. For this to have happened during his time, oh it must hurt. To see them taking the Museum apart. All that work. At the beginning, I've been told people like him were sought out, given fat payments. Those who could remember the objects, and partial fragments of the catalogue, from the old Museum. They were then, once in, teased and tortured into a pool of facts and memories that could be trusted. And when that appeared too lean, others were sought. Others who hadn't been so badly harmed, who could help recreate a history culture, to explicitly connect those two things. To bring back to life the unforeseen, unknown, unintelligible, almost unthinkable, into a massive throbbing establishment. One so amazing to witness that no visitor could get to asking whether it was genuine. The pasts reanimated before they were forever forgotten. Thought up by these obviously important people, who in their renovations, after a time, when the eye became lax, allowed new interpretations of their history. Where is that now? He must be thinking, this second son of a creative administrator. Well, it's on a dish on a plate.

The curator's voice is stuck. He doesn't want to know that this is the time when every object will be demolished down to its atoms. Each thing will be removed, uncatalogued, and then vapourised. Then each brick of this place, made dust. And all will be buried. Well, I assume. With no more things and no more visitors, he must be asking himself, if the building lies empty, is it a Museum at all?

A visitor goes to attack me as I watch. They lunge and grab at my plain white undershirt like an amateur. I catch their closing hand in my own. I use my free hand, still checking the curator and his party, to prop up this visitor's arm, and in one sudden motion, snap a wrist bone. As the person begins to react, their body open to me, I just hit them in the throat and return to my watching. I don't need to kill anyone. That is in the past. I have nothing to prove. I have learned to just leave it be. The curator's hesitation, however, is less wise, and a sign of his inability to adapt to times of change. Makes sense. In the end, soon after, it is the guards behind him who shove him forcefully into a crowd of coursing visitors. It's hardly a surprise, an almost uninteresting betrayal, as of course, now is the traditional time for revenge. An ending much like the slaughtering of a living creature for food. As in the way a cow's neck is cut or a chicken's neck is snapped. This slice of the crowd, itself mortally wounded, hounded, and staggering like the infirm, seizes him. He becomes like scraps of meat and his beautiful clothes are destroyed. Their provincial visitor faces show no sign they know whom it is they are killing. I feel in my pocket for my dainty little flute of a warclub.

I turn away from these incidents and see Greg, Rebecca and a group of guards in a purposeful unit, moving through the crowds, with excellent weapons. They have maces, morning stars, blades and even guns, though they seem to be saving bullets. For later? Or for themselves? I am not inclined to join them. They are pulling down one of the large advertising banners and stringing up a giant poster of their own. It has things to say, written in paint, slogans. That's that then. I attempt to read it. The words are really well painted, written, and even have quotation marks. Excellent penmanship. This banner is being hoisted thirty feet in the air, high above the people. To proclaim, silently. I see older visitors squinting to read it too, if they are not being scratched or hit as it unfurls, of course. I turn away. This is not the time to be distracted by reading. I've heard it all before, probably, and you never know how persuasive some mantras can be. They have a mind of their own. And anyway, now I know what is what, I just want to avoid any personal messiness.

Greg's team moves from the banner and begins to charge into the mass, picking on those they don't want. The visitors who do not like to be told what to do, that have their pride hurt by boundaries of any kind, are being rinsed. Oh yes, I think, how nice. What an accomplishment for those who have made it to the end. What pride they take in their liquidated state. Alone is not far away, at last. To be with nobody and nothing. No bunking. The barracks will be burned to ash, and so uninhabitable. The wings will be destroyed. A shift in the crowds, and I see the people pouring out of the doors and stairs and corridors and upper floors and lower, all fighting with each other still, inexhaustible, screaming and stabbing and being attacked and attacking and hosts hair being ripped out and guard's necks being squeezed and I do understand absolutely what's escaping. I think of the near endless galleries that must be being pulled down, the cases smashed, the glass shoved back into ancient things by bleeding hands. It is an effigy, after all. And this commentary is an act of survival. Head down, penetrating, pitiless in times of great difficulty, sensible to have brought myself into the Museum, for my own sake. But no point crying over spilt milk. Things vary. No big deal. A big messy reset. Now it is time again to find a nice hole to dig, to become something out in the fields. To go back to when things were and not made for commentary. For me, this has been the worst place in the world. But only because it insisted, I forgot other places were there, and it is often home which is worst.

I am at once capable of doing anything. I begin to shout as loud as I can. The Museum is closed. Make your way to the exits. The people make to leave and I find myself thinking loosely it is a wonder.

XV

Between 6am and 8am, the end features collapsing columns, and water, unexpectedly, flooding in from surroundings, causing a minor eclipse, indoors, as from a lake burst or relentless rains. The masonry begins to crumble. The small galleries go down first. The trampling hoof of the flood washes all the panicking mass. The planned escapees don't necessarily do so. This is a reverse black day, a sell on air and running fast. Waves pour and envelope the spaces like an undercloud. Waterspace is no longer peopled. All fires are extinguished. There is no sense this is planned.

Space breaks in; a celestial, murk space that is no longer happening in time. To most, the empty space turns as obscure as deep water. Destruction escalates beyond a surge and gets out of hand. More plans depart. Things can't grow.

Survivors climb to high ground and eat with such anger. They struggle with each other and the thing that fills the land becomes one colour, one colour between colours, a sand of sorts, that is disappearing and being refilled. A stupid call to surviving comes first. They realise it is no longer possible for anything to studied.

A billowing mouth of earth that was once the Museum seems full, as its levels break and into the basement drains the major body of the flood. It's a sinkhole, a big lost gap, a tunnel down to almost no solid matter, let alone history. The hole seems not to stop its chewing and swallowing. A mouth free, a few necks bobbing, bulging, still trailing down, like a chin, wiped. Then a kind of music, without it. No building means no objects to look at, and no public. Lovely to our above ground ears, somewhere suspended, in a gloam place. Bells ring.

Finally, things in time are free to just sit there, unwatched.

Steven J Fowler is a writer and poet living in London. His collections include *Fights* (Veer Books, 2011), *The Rottweiler's Guide to the Dog Owner* (Eyewear Books, 2014), *{Enthusiasm}* (Test Centre, 2015), *The Guide to Being Bear Aware* (Shearsman Books, 2017), *I will show you the life of the mind (on prescription drugs)* (Dostoyevsky Wannabe, 2020) and *The Great Apes* (Broken Sleep Books, 2022). His work has become known for its exploration of the potential of poetry, alongside collaboration, curation, asemic writing, sound poetry, concrete poetry, and performance. He has been commissioned by institutions such as the Tate Modern, The Photographer's Gallery, Wellcome Collection and Southbank Centre, and he has presented his work at over fifty international festivals, including Hay Xalapa, Mexico; Dhaka Lit Fest; Hay Arequipa, Peru; and the Niniti Festival, Iraq. Fowler was nominated for the White Review Short Story Prize, 2014, and his short stories have appeared in anthologies, such as Isabel Waidner's edited collection, *Liberating the Canon* (Dostoyevsky Wannabe, 2018).

Coincidentally—from December 2007 to November 2014 —Fowler was a guard, or 'visitor host,' in the employ of the British Museum. This book is dedicated to his colleagues, living and dead.

MUEUM
SJ Fowler

This edition was first published in Great Britain by Tenement
Press, 2022, and edited by Dominic J. Jaeckle. *MUEUM* was
designed and typeset by Traven T. Croves (Matthew Stuart &
Andrew Walsh-Lister).

Chapter VII is an expansion of a fiction, also titled 'Mueum,'
which was shortlisted for the White Review Short Story
Prize, 2014.

Stickered editions carry a reproduction of a photograph
of Fowler 'on shift' at the British Museum (see also, p. 148),
Alexander Kell, © 2014.

A CIP record for this publication is available from the
British Library.

Tenement Press 4, MMXXII
ISBN 978-1-8380200-6-4

Printed and bound by Lulu.
Typeset in Arnhem Pro Blond.

Tenement Press is an occasional publisher of esoteric;
experimental;
accidental;
and interdisciplinary literatures.

www.tenementpress.com
editors@tenementpress.com